FORBIDDEN MATE

FORBIDDEN #7

R.L. KENDERSON

FORBIDDEN MATE

QUENTIN RAWLING EXITED the gate at the Minneapolis-St. Paul International Airport and headed down to baggage claim. He hadn't realized how much he had missed Minneapolis until his plane landed. While he had been glad that he could help his sister and parents by going with her to the rehab facility in Switzerland, he was happy to be home.

For the last month of his sister's yearlong treatment, she was in the center, alone. Patients did this to learn to rely on themselves and to trust that they could make good decisions on their own. Or something like that. But it only happened if the patients were doing well in treatment, which his sister was.

So, while Larissa had one month left before she would come back, Quentin was home a month earlier than he'd originally thought when he left the country.

His phone buzzed in his pocket.

Jeremiah: I'm here, waiting for you.

Quentin grinned down at his phone.

While Switzerland was beautiful and had many English speakers, he'd felt lonely and like an outsider. He saw his sister every day, but she was regularly tied up with her treatment, so he often had hours to himself.

It took him less than a week to find a local coffee shop and become a regular. While the workers and other customers became acquaintances of his and people he could bullshit with, none of them were true friends. And Quentin started feeling homesick.

About two months in, he was sitting in his usual spot when he heard an American accent. Not only was the guy an American, but he was also from Minnesota and a wolf-shifter. Just like Quentin.

Normally, he probably wouldn't have been so bold, but the second the guy was handed his order, Quentin approached him.

And that was how he'd met Jeremiah.

Jeremiah had gotten to the treatment facility with his mother—supporting her the same way Quentin supported his sister—a month and a half before Quentin. It was kind of crazy that it had taken them two months to run into each other.

Unfortunately, because Jeremiah had arrived a month and a half prior to Quentin, this meant he had gone back home a month and a half earlier, too, as his mom had also done well in treatment. The last few weeks had been hard on Quentin, even with his sister having more and more free time.

Quentin: I'll be out as soon as I grab my luggage.

"Hey."

Quentin looked up to see Jeremiah standing five feet away. His dark hair was cut shorter than the last time Quentin had seen him, but his green eyes exuded the same warmth he remembered.

Quentin broke out in a grin as he hurried to Jeremiah and hugged him. "I thought you were going to wait in the car."

Jeremiah smiled and shook his head. "I wanted to see you as soon as possible."

"I missed you," Quentin said with a sigh.

"I missed you, too."

Quentin grabbed the front of Jeremiah's shirt and yanked him close, so he could kiss him. He smiled against the other man's mouth. "Thanks for coming to pick me up."

He let go of Jeremiah's shirt and headed for the baggage carousel.

"You know I wouldn't have missed it. I needed a break from my mother."

"How's she doing?"

Jeremiah's mom had been home for two weeks. She had been alone at the center the last month, too, but her treatment was done now, and Quentin imagined it must have been an adjustment for her, being back in the States.

"Good. I made sure to clean out her house before she got back to Minnesota. No liquor anywhere. The only problem now is, she doesn't have anything to do. Drinking was her only hobby." Jeremiah rolled his eyes. "And now, it's hanging out with her son. I would have come to the airport no matter what, so I could get some time away."

Quentin laughed. "You'll have to help her find some new friends and things to do. I'm sure there's a senior center not too far from her house somewhere."

Jeremiah scratched his chin. "She said absolutely no bingo."

"Senior centers do more than just bingo. Some can even help people find places to volunteer."

Jeremiah dropped his hand. "Thanks. How do you know all this anyway?"

"It's part of the job."

"Which one?"

Quentin thought about it for a second. "Both."

Even with finding Jeremiah in Europe, he had still felt like a piece of himself was missing while he was there. His work. He loved being a sentinel, and he loved being a police officer. He couldn't wait to get back to both his jobs.

"Is that your suitcase?" Jeremiah asked, pointing to a large black one coming down the chute.

"How'd you know?" Quentin joked.

"It's the only suitcase big enough to hold months' worth of clothes."

Quentin pulled his luggage off the carousel with ease. "Yet it felt like I was doing laundry every other day."

"Same."

Quentin smiled. "Lead the way to your car."

"This way," Jeremiah said, pointing to one of the double doors.

Quentin noticed that Jeremiah's mood had suddenly changed. "You okay?"

Jeremiah took a deep breath. "Yeah. Super nervous about meeting the alpha."

That would explain it.

"I told you, Damien is cool. He's young and progressive. You don't have to be worried."

"Easier said than done."

"You'll see when we get there."

"Is there anyone I need to be worried about?"

An image of Hunter flashed through Quentin's brain, but he immediately pushed the vampire from his mind. Hunter didn't want to be with him, so he shouldn't have a problem with Quentin bringing someone home.

"Nope," Quentin told Jeremiah. "Everyone's super cool, and they already know I'm gay. They're going to love you."

TWO

HUNTER ESMUND SLAPPED his hand down on his thigh. He couldn't stop pumping his leg up and down as nerves racked his body, and sooner or later, someone was going to notice.

But it didn't stop him from feeling anxious as hell, and he stood up from the chair he had been occupying in the back of the room. He was way too restless to sit still.

After eleven long months, he was going to see Quentin again.

Hunter hadn't realized that, during the last month of Quentin's sister's year of treatment, his sister would be on her own. So, when Hunter had found out Quentin was coming home a month earlier than he'd expected, he hadn't been prepared for all his emotions to hit him. He was excited and nervous, and the anticipation was killing him.

The welcome-home gathering in the wolf-shifter home included the wolf-shifter alpha, Damien Lowell, and his mate, Payton. It was a full house with all the wolf-shifter sentinels, plus a few more, like Quentin's parents.

Yet Hunter felt like he was all alone.

No one could understand how he was feeling.

To say Hunter's relationship with Quentin was complicated would be simplifying it.

Hunter had always thought there was something wrong with him because he didn't care for sex. Quentin had opened his eyes to the fact that he was wrong. It wasn't that he didn't like sex. He just didn't like having sex with women.

Knowing the truth about himself was a blessing and a curse. The sexual part of himself felt free and satisfied for the first time. But now, he also felt more trapped than ever.

As a Guardian for the vampire species, he feared he would lose his position, his fellow Guardians, and his own family if they found out he was gay.

So, despite being hopelessly in love with Quentin, Hunter had told the wolf-shifter they couldn't be in a relationship. Not even after Quentin told Hunter he was leaving for a year. Not even after Hunter let Quentin have sex with him before he left the country.

To this day, Quentin was still the only male he'd had sex with.

And now, Quentin was back.

And no one knew the torment that was troubling Hunter at the thought of seeing Quentin again.

"I think he's here," Payton announced from her position by the front window.

"Turn off the lights," Damien called out, and the house was plunged into darkness as someone flipped the switch.

The loud voices that had filled the room moments before were now whispers, as everyone was trying to stay silent in order to surprise Quentin when he came through the door.

A small wail sounded, and Isabelle made soothing noises to quiet her baby. Isabelle was a wolf-shifter mated to Zane, a cat-shifter. Zane lived with the wolf-shifters as a liaison, as did Hunter, but tonight, Zane was on duty. The cat-shifters had doubled up on their shifts so that all the wolf-shifter sentinels could be there to celebrate Quentin's return. That left Isabelle alone to take care of the four-month-old, but she managed to soothe baby Kat.

Zane thought her name was ironic.

Hunter thought it was stupid, but she wasn't his kid.

Of course, that could be the bitterness and loneliness speaking.

"I heard that Quentin was bringing home a surprise," Raven whispered to Kendall.

Kendall rubbed her round belly and said, "I hope it's Swiss chocolate."

Raven snorted.

"Hey, the baby wants what it wants," Kendall defended herself.

Kendall normally lived with the cat-shifters—she had traded spots with Zane—but she wasn't allowed to be on duty, so she had recently moved back in with the wolf-shifters for the duration of her pregnancy.

"You know, if you told Eldon about the baby, he'd probably go out and get you chocolate, like any father-to-be," Raven pointed out.

Kendall sighed. "I will tell him. When I'm ready. Besides, we agreed to stay apart, so no one would know that I was part of getting his brother arrested."

"That was months ago. I think you're safe to tell the *father of your baby* that you're pregnant."

"Quentin had better have brought chocolate, or I'm going to regret coming over here," Kendall grumbled.

"I just care about you, is all," Raven said.

"*Shh,*" Chase said. "Will you two stop fighting? Kendall will tell Eldon when she's ready."

"Thank you, Chase," Kendall said.

Ranulf growled, "Will you all shut the fuck up? Quentin just got out of the car."

"Dick," Raven muttered under her breath.

Hunter chuckled silently, feeling a little better after listening to the wolf-shifters bicker.

But the momentary relief disappeared as soon as the door opened.

Someone turned on the lights in the living room, and everyone shouted, "Welcome home."

Everyone but Hunter.

His voice was stuck in the back of his throat as he stared at Quentin.

The wolf-shifter looked different.

He was even bigger than when he'd left Minnesota. His biceps looked like they wanted to escape his shirtsleeves. His normally short black hair was longer than when Hunter had last seen him. But the biggest changes were that Quentin's brown eyes were shining, and he had a grin splitting across his face.

Because the wolf-shifter wasn't alone. A handsome male stood next to him with a timid smile on his face. But the worst part was, his hand was in Quentin's.

Quentin's surprise was—

"Ooh, Quentin has a boyfriend," Raven said.

"Boo. I wanted chocolate," Kendall said.

And Hunter wanted to be anywhere but there.

He prayed the floor would open up and swallow him down.

THREE

KENDALL WALKER WAS PRACTICALLY KNOCKED off her feet as Hunter blew past her. Thankfully, Raven caught her before she fell on her ass. Her damn belly had been throwing her balance off for the last few months.

Kendall turned to look just as Hunter's dirty-blond hair disappeared out the back door.

"What's that about?" Raven asked. "Hunter's usually more polite than that."

Kendall shrugged. "I have no idea."

Chase and Ranulf exchanged looks.

Raven put her hands on her hips and narrowed her brown eyes. "What do you two know that no one else does?"

The two males looked at each other again. Ranulf shrugged.

Chase looked back at Kendall and Raven. "If I tell you, can you keep it between us?"

"Gee, I don't know if I can keep a secret," Kendall said, her voice dripping with sarcasm.

Chase glanced down at her stomach. "Not all of us have secret babies, Kendall."

"I was referring to our existence, our jobs as sentinels. Things like that, asshole."

Raven rolled her eyes. "Children, can we not fight?"

"He started it," Kendall mumbled.

She never got this much crap with the cat-shifters. They understood that she was going to tell Eldon when she was ready. She had promised she was going to do it before the baby was born. And she would. She just hadn't felt the time was right yet.

This time, Ranulf rolled his eyes. "Quentin and Hunter have been involved in the past."

Kendall's jaw dropped. "No way."

"You're full of shit," Raven said.

Chase shook his head, his unusual orange eyes serious. "No joking."

Raven tilted her head. "How do the two of you know?" she asked in disbelief.

"Trust us, we know," Chase said.

Kendall smiled. "I know how they know."

"Oh?" Raven raised an eyebrow. "Do tell."

"Because they've been involved with each other. Just like Quentin and Hunter."

Ranulf smirked, and Chase held up his hands.

"Hold up. We are nothing like Quentin and Hunter. We do not deny our feelings for each other." Chase wrapped his arm around Ranulf. "And while we've had sex with the same female at the same time, we've never had sex with each other."

Raven squirmed, and Kendall glanced at her friend. Raven didn't return the look.

Kendall turned back to the two males. "How do you know you wouldn't like to have sex with each other? Maybe you just like having sex with the same woman because you can't admit how you feel about each other."

Ranulf snorted. "Because Chase is a horrible kisser."

Chase dropped his arm. "I am not," he said to his best friend. "Listen, ladies, a female once dared us to kiss while we were having sex with her. We did. Neither of us liked it." He narrowed his eyes at Ranulf. "But it wasn't because I'm a bad kisser."

Ranulf lifted a shoulder in a casual shrug.

Chase clenched his jaw. "Maybe you're the bad kisser. Did you ever think of that?"

Ranulf shook his head and laughed. "Dude, I'm messing with you."

"Oh." Chase lifted his chin. "Told you I'm a great kisser."

"All I'm admitting to is you not being a bad kisser. I never said you were great at it," Ranulf said, not done giving the other male shit. "But Chase is right. We aren't like Quentin and Hunter. Truthfully, if I could mate with Chase, I would. But I'm just not attracted to him like that."

Chase clapped his hands in front of his chest and batted his eyelashes. "Oh, Ranulf. I love you, too. If you had a pussy, I'd mate with you, too." He grabbed Ranulf's hand. "Will you be my non-sexual life partner?"

Ranulf rolled his blue-green eyes. "I'm going to go say hi to Quentin." He turned and walked away.

Chase frowned. "Was that a no?"

Kendall smacked him on the side of the arm. "Sucks to be you." She nudged Raven with her elbow. "Let's welcome Quentin home."

Raven followed Kendall, and Kendall looked at the dark-haired female over her shoulder. "You thinking about having a threesome with those two?"

Raven scowled. "Never."

Kendall smirked. She didn't believe that for a second.

FOUR

QUENTIN'S PARENTS excused themselves to go and pick up some food, and then he saw Ranulf, Kendall, and Raven coming over to him.

He grabbed Ranulf's hand and pulled the other male in for a hug.

Ranulf smacked his back. "It's good to have you home."

"It's good to be back."

The two stepped back. Quentin hugged Raven and then Kendall.

When Kendall pulled away, Quentin looked down at her growing abdomen. "What is going on here? No one told me you were pregnant." And he'd kept in contact with Damien regularly.

Kendall's smile dropped. "I'm not pregnant. I'm just fat. Thanks for pointing that out, Quentin."

He laughed. "Nice try. I can smell the baby on you."

"Nuts. I was hoping with all the different smells in the room, I'd be able to fool you."

"That's a cruel joke."

Kendall shrugged.

"Now, seriously, why didn't anyone tell me?"

"Because Kendall's in denial," Raven said. "She's trying to pretend she didn't have sex with a cat-shifter and get knocked up."

"I am not," Kendall protested.

"Whatever."

"Speaking of no one telling anyone anything, who's your friend?" Kendall asked, effectively changing the subject.

Quentin squeezed Jeremiah's hand. "This is Jeremiah. We met in Switzerland and became friends when we realized we were both from Minnesota."

Raven raised her brow. "Looks like you're more than friends to me."

Quentin smiled. "Yeah, you could say that."

Everyone laughed.

"Jeremiah, this is Ranulf, Raven, and Kendall." Quentin looked up to see Chase joining them. "And this is Chase."

Chase lifted a hand.

"Chase, this is Jeremiah."

"Hey, Jeremiah." Chase pulled Quentin into a hug. "It's good to have you back."

"Thanks, man."

The six of them talked for a while before everyone moved on to mingle more, except Kendall. She looked like she wanted to say something.

"What?" Quentin asked her.

"Did you by chance bring any chocolate?" She smiled. "You know, Swiss chocolate."

Jeremiah laughed. "Where's the bathroom?"

Quentin pointed him in the direction and turned to Kendall. "I might have brought some back with me."

Kendall clapped. "*Yes.*"

"It's in my suitcase, but I'll try to remember to get you some before the night is over."

She put a hand on his arm. "Thank you."

"You're welcome."

Kendall turned to walk away, but Quentin grabbed her wrist.

She lifted her brows in surprise.

Quentin looked around before lowering his voice. "Did I see that Hunter was here?"

As crazy as it was, with all the shifters in the room, Quentin also thought he'd smelled the vampire. But he hadn't seen Hunter, except for the possible first glance he'd gotten when he walked into the house.

Kendall's eyes filled with sympathy. "Um…he was here, but he took off soon after you arrived."

Quentin dropped her arm. "I see."

"I know you two have a past." She lifted a shoulder. "Maybe he didn't know what to say to you."

Quentin narrowed his eyes. "I don't know what you know or what you think you know, but you can't say anything. Vampires are not open-minded."

"Naya is."

"Naya is the exception, not the rule."

Kendall nodded. "I understand. I'll spread the word."

Panic raced through his body. "Who else knows?"

Kendall cursed under her breath. "I didn't mean to worry you. Just a few of us. And nobody has said anything so far. I'll make sure they continue to keep their mouths closed."

Quentin took a deep breath. "Thank you."

If Hunter's life were ruined because of him, he'd never forgive himself. As much as Hunter's rejection hurt, Quentin still cared very deeply for the vampire and wished him nothing but peace.

Kendall made a quick glance as Jeremiah walked back to the two of them. "If I see Hunter, I'll let you know," she said quickly.

Quentin gave her a small smile. "Thank you." He was also thanking her for not saying anything in front of Jeremiah. Quentin hadn't quite told him everything about Hunter and their past.

"Hey," Jeremiah said when he reached Quentin and Kendall. "You two still talking about chocolate?"

God bless Kendall. She didn't act suspicious. Instead, she laughed. "I might be craving sweets, but I don't think I could carry on a conversation that long about chocolate, Swiss or not. No, I was telling Quentin he should show you around."

"And I was just agreeing with her," Quentin said.

FIVE

HUNTER THREW BACK his fifth beer and frowned. He was never going to get drunk, thanks to his stupidly fast metabolism. He needed something stronger.

He pushed himself to his feet, leaving the booth he'd been sitting in at the back of the bar. He didn't want to wait around for the waitress to show up. He needed more alcohol. Now.

Unfortunately, no matter how much he drank, he'd probably never get rid of the image of Quentin holding hands with that guy.

But that wasn't going to stop Hunter from trying.

He was almost to the counter when a random asshole bumped into him. Not in a helping mood, Hunter stepped around the guy and continued on. Unfortunately for the guy, Hunter was what had been holding him up, and the guy fell on his ass.

Hunter chuckled as he reached the bartender.

"What can I get you?"

"Five shots of whiskey. Make it the cheapest brand you have." He wanted to feel it burn all the way to his stomach.

The bartender raised an eyebrow but didn't question Hunter's choice.

"Hey."

Hunter heard a voice from behind him, but he didn't turn around. He'd come alone, and someone was most likely speaking to a friend.

"*Hey.*"

The bartender nodded his head as he lined up shot glasses. "I think he's talking to you."

Hunter sighed and turned around.

It was the guy who had run into him.

Hunter didn't say anything.

"I fell because of you."

"No. You fell because you're drunk."

"You could have caught me."

Hunter lifted a shoulder. "I don't owe you anything."

The guy scoffed, "It's called being a decent human being."

"I'm not decent." *Or a human being.* "Not tonight anyway."

Hunter might have been acting nonchalant, but deep inside, he really wanted the guy to throw a punch. If the stupid human hit him first, he'd have no choice but to defend himself. Maybe if he pushed the asshole's buttons a little more...

"You want someone to hold your hand so you don't fall next time, go find your mommy." Hunter couldn't stop the smile from slipping onto his face as he turned his back to the guy.

"Motherfucker," he heard the guy mutter, and Hunter braced for impact.

Unfortunately, a bouncer stepped in at the last second and stopped the guy.

"Get him out of here," the bartender said to the bouncer. He looked at Hunter and slid the shots over. "Sorry about that. Thanks for not hitting the guy. It's always a mess when there's a fight in here."

Hunter picked up the first shot and knocked it back. He pulled out his wallet and left the guy a big tip out of guilt. He hadn't been thinking about anyone but himself when he tried to get the guy to punch him. "Thanks for the shots."

He picked up the remaining four in his hands and carried them back to the table.

His server showed up at the same time. "I was going to ask if you needed anything else, but it looks like you got it taken care of," she said.

"Actually, you can bring me another beer."

"Make that two," said some man Hunter had never seen before.

The guy had dark, shaggy hair and looked like he'd had a rough life.

The server smiled. "Two beers. I'll be right back with those."

The man sat down across from Hunter.

"Who the fuck are you?" Hunter asked.

He lifted a glass to his lips and threw the shot back. As he lowered the glass, he inhaled deeply. The guy was a wolf-shifter.

"I'm Trey."

Hunter downed another shot in one swallow. "And?"

Trey glanced at the table. "And you look like you might need something a little stronger than alcohol."

The waitress returned with their drinks before Hunter could answer.

"I got it," Trey said.

Hunter threw his money down on the tray before the wolf-shifter could get his money out. "I'll pay for myself." He didn't want to owe the guy anything.

Trey shrugged. "Suit yourself." He set more money on the tray. "Keep the change," he told the server.

As soon as she was out of earshot, Hunter said, "Listen,

whatever it is you're trying to sell, I'm not buying. I don't do hard drugs." He might be in the mood to get shit-faced tonight, but he wasn't going to do anything to risk his job.

Trey leaned in close. "I'm not talking about drugs."

Hunter drank his second to last shot. "Oh?"

Later—much later—he would kick himself for asking, but in the moment, his curiosity was piqued. If something could help the burning hole in his chest, he'd take it.

"I noticed you with that human over there."

Hunter snorted. "What about him?"

"You wanted to fight him."

Figuring there was no point in denying it, he shrugged. "Yeah. So what?"

"What if I could take you somewhere that you could fight? You can get out whatever's bothering you, and you don't have to worry about the cops, sentinels, or Guardians."

Hunter snorted.

"And no humans. Shifters and vamps only. You don't have to fear you might kill some weakling."

"And what's in it for you?"

The guy reclined back and stretched his arms out on the top of the booth. "Maybe I just like helping others."

"Bullshit."

Trey laughed. "Okay, so maybe some friends and I place bets on who's going to win."

"And if I fight and you lose a bet?"

"Then, I lose a bet. You don't owe me anything." He dropped his arms and leaned forward again. "You interested?"

Hunter's rational self was screaming at him to say no.

"Yeah. Count me in."

Trey grinned. "Well, all right. Let's go. I'll drive."

Hunter swallowed his last shot and slammed the glass down on the table. "I'll drive myself. I don't trust you for shit."

The guy looked down at the empty shot glasses.

Hunter had a mild buzz but was far from drunk. If he were lucky, he'd get pulled over and have to spend the night in jail. He wouldn't have to worry about going home and seeing Quentin then.

The guy raised his gaze back to Hunter. "Fine. Follow me then."

SIX

RAVEN KALE WENT around the house, picking up plates and glasses that had been left lying on tables and counters. Apparently, some shifters didn't know what a wastebasket was.

"Hey. Do you care if I go to bed?"

She turned around to say good-bye to Kendall. "Not at all."

Kendall threw a stack of paper plates in the garbage can near the end of the counter. "Thanks. I haven't been sleeping well, and I'm tired."

"I understand. Thanks for helping me clean up." Raven put her hand on her hip.

Chase and Ranulf walked into the kitchen.

Chase was holding a trash bag. "I think we got everything."

"Anything else can wait until morning," Ranulf said. "I'm going to bed."

Chase opened the back door and threw the sack into the bin outside. "Me, too." He closed the back door. "See you ladies in the morning."

"Night, guys," Kendall said.

The males left the room, and Raven wrapped up a tray of

food that had been sitting on the counter and put it in the fridge. "I'm going to bed, too. I'm hoping to get a good night's sleep before I'm on duty tomorrow."

Kendall pushed out her lip. "I miss being on duty."

Raven glanced down at Kendall's pregnant belly. "You'll be back to work before you know it. Enjoy your time off."

Kendall scoffed, "Easier said than done."

Raven sympathized. She wouldn't like to be on the sidelines either. It was a good thing she didn't have a mate and wouldn't get pregnant for many more years. Maybe never. "Why don't you and I make some time to go do something together? I can't put you to work, but I can get you out of the house."

"That sounds heavenly."

"Now that Quentin is back, we'll all have extra days off, so you and I can hang out more."

Instead of looking happy, Kendall bit her lip in worry.

"What's wrong?"

"I forgot to tell you what Quentin said."

"What did he say?"

"He wanted to make sure that no one said anything about him and Hunter being involved. Vampires are more closed-minded than us."

Raven frowned. "I would never say anything."

"I know. I'm simply passing the message along. And I know you won't, but what about Chase and Ranulf?"

Raven lifted a brow.

Kendall chuckled. "Okay, what about Chase?"

Ranulf was the quieter of the two males and probably wouldn't say anything to anyone. Chase, on the other hand, was a talker. Not necessarily about secrets, but one could never be too careful.

Kendall yawned. "I'd better go say something to them before I forget again."

Raven squeezed her friend's arm. "You go to bed and get

some sleep. I'll go tell them. I wouldn't worry too much because they've already known this secret for a while now."

"Except they both told us."

Raven smiled. "Exactly."

Kendall rolled her eyes.

Raven laughed. "Go to bed. I won't forget."

"Thanks, lady."

"Anytime."

Kendall headed upstairs, and Raven wiped down the counters in the kitchen before going up, too.

With Kendall moving back in, the shifters had done some bedroom switching since Zane and Isabelle had taken her old room. Ranulf and Chase had volunteered to share a room, so Damien and Payton had decided to give them the master, which had the most space for Ranulf's and Chase's beds and all their stuff, and they'd moved into Ranulf's. Kendall had taken Chase's bedroom, which was at the end of the hall, next to the master.

It was a good thing that Chase and Ranulf got along so well because Raven doubted that Kendall was going to go back and live with the cat-shifters after the baby was born. She wasn't going to be able to work at first, and after that, she'd have an infant. It wouldn't be fair for the cats to help take care of her wolf baby. Even if the baby was half-cat-shifter, the father was not a sentinel.

Odds were, either she, Chase, or Ranulf would offer up to live with the cats once everything was decided. And since Chase and Ranulf were attached at the hip, Raven was betting she'd be the one to go.

She didn't hate the idea, but she wasn't excited about it either. She liked her home.

Ranulf and Chase's door was shut, so Raven tapped her knuckles on the wood.

"Come in."

Raven opened the door to see Chase lying on his bed in shorts and no shirt, looking at his phone. "What's up?" he asked without bothering to glance her way.

Raven scanned the room. "Where's Ranulf?"

The master bath opened, and a lighter-haired wolf walked out with a towel wrapped around his waist. "I'm here."

Chase put his cell down, and it suddenly dawned on her that she was alone in the room of two very good-looking males, and knowing the two liked to have sex with the same woman at the same time seemed to be all she could think about at the moment.

Raven had participated in a threesome once before and told herself never again. The two men she'd been with seemed to think they were in some porno, and the sex had been all about them. Part of it was her fault. In her fantasies, she'd imagined the two males pleasuring her, which wasn't fair either. But if the two guys had been willing to meet her halfway, she probably would have walked away somewhat satisfied. In the end, it hadn't been good. It hadn't even been okay. She much preferred one-on-one or solo acts.

"Raven?"

She looked over at Ranulf and shook her head to clear it. "Sorry. I just came to let you know that Kendall talked with Quentin. He wants to make sure we keep his relationship with Hunter to ourselves. He doesn't want the vampires finding out."

Ranulf walked to his dresser and opened a couple of drawers. "Would they punish him?"

"I don't know," Raven answered. "Maybe. They are more conservative than us when it comes to sex."

Ranulf dropped his towel, and Raven's eyes narrowed in on his very nice ass.

"Quentin doesn't have to worry. We wouldn't do that to

him or Hunter," Chase said, and Raven pulled her eyes away from Ranulf.

Chase lifted his phone back up, and with his free hand, he ran his hand down his built chest and muscular stomach.

Gah. What is wrong with me? She needed to stop it before her scent changed and the two males knew she was thinking about sex. With them.

But it was too late. As if in slow motion, Ranulf turned around, and Chase lowered his arm. The two of them stared at her and then exchanged looks with each other.

Chase grinned as he looked back at her. "Raven, are you thinking about sex?"

She straightened her spine. There was no point in lying to a shifter, so she might as well own it. "I've been feeling horny lately. So what?"

Ranulf rubbed his chin. "Nah. You're thinking about having sex with us."

Raven rolled her eyes. "I've had sex with two men. Not worth it."

Chase tsked teasingly. "We've told you, it's because you've never had sex with the two of us."

"Both of you need to check your egos. You're not that good."

"Come over here and find out," Ranulf said.

While Chase was smiling, Ranulf's expression was serious. She thought he was joking, but since he had such a poker face, she couldn't tell.

Not that she was going to find out.

"That's my cue to go to bed." Raven turned around before she changed her mind.

"You can run, but you can't hide," Chase taunted as she walked into her room and shut the door.

She took a deep breath and went in search of her vibrator.

SEVEN

QUENTIN SCROLLED through the news app on his phone, but he wasn't really paying it any attention. He was too busy waiting for Hunter to come home. He almost wished he smoked so that he had a reason to be sitting on the stairs of the back porch like a pathetic loser, but he would have to settle with looking at his cell.

His ears perked as he caught the sound of a vehicle coming down the driveway. The garage and driveway were off to the side of the house, so he couldn't see whose car was pulling up.

Two minutes later, he was disappointed to see that it was Zane.

"Hey, man," the cat-shifter said.

"Hey."

Zane held out his hand, and Quentin clasped it.

"Sorry I missed your party."

Quentin smiled. "I understand. Someone's got to work around here."

"I bet it's good to be home."

"It is. Switzerland was beautiful, but there really is no place like home."

Zane's phone buzzed, and he pulled it from his back pocket. "Speaking of home, the wifey is wondering where I am."

Zane was about the only shifter Quentin knew who would call his mate wifey.

Quentin waved Zane toward the door. "Go. We can catch up later."

Zane walked up the few stairs and slapped Quentin on the back. "It's good to have you back."

"Thanks," Quentin said, but Zane was already closing the door.

"What are you doing out here?"

Quentin's head swung around at the sound of Hunter's voice.

"Waiting for you."

Hunter stepped partly into the light, but Quentin could only see the lower half of his face. It was enough to catch Hunter's smirk.

"Your boyfriend okay with that? I thought you'd be upstairs in bed with him."

The bitterness in Hunter's voice was like a razor to Quentin. He wanted to reach out and comfort the vampire, but it wasn't Quentin's fault they weren't together.

"He went home."

Jeremiah had wanted to stay, but Quentin had made some excuse as to why he didn't want to have sex with everyone around. While it was true that he usually didn't bring guys home to the house, he hadn't had any problem fucking Hunter in his room upstairs before he left for Europe.

"And he's not my boyfriend."

Quentin was beginning to think he was as fucked in the head as Hunter. He had a great guy—a fellow wolf-shifter—who liked him a lot. But he hadn't fully committed himself to Jeremiah. They'd only had each other in Europe—almost like they were living in their own little bubble—so they'd mutually decided they should wait at least a couple of weeks after they were back home before deciding if being exclusive was what they both wanted.

If Quentin knew what was good for him, he'd march inside, call Jeremiah, and beg him to be exclusive.

But when it came to Hunter, he didn't know what was good for him.

"Oh, so you hold hands with all random men?"

"Don't be an asshole. It doesn't suit you."

Hunter snorted.

"Yes, I am dating Jeremiah, but we're taking it slow."

"Are you fucking him?" Hunter paused. "Is he fucking you?"

Quentin shook his head. Not to say no, but to let Hunter know, "That's none of your fucking business." But if he were to answer the vampire, he'd admit that, yes, he was fucking Jeremiah, but not the other way around. Quentin hadn't let anyone take his ass in years, and he wasn't going to start with Jeremiah.

"Right. Of course you are." Hunter lowered his head as his shoulders sagged.

Quentin had to stop himself from pulling Hunter into his arms.

"Is that why you didn't stick around for my welcome-home party? You bailed before we could even say hello."

Hunter lifted his head and his chin. "Don't flatter yourself."

Quentin raised his eyebrows. "You've turned mean since I last saw you."

Hunter shrugged. "Yeah, maybe." He looked up at the sky. It was still dark, but dawn would be there soon. "I should go inside."

"After you." Quentin gestured toward the house.

Hunter stood there, as if waiting for Quentin to go in first, but he didn't even get up from his spot on the steps.

The vampire cussed under his breath and stepped toward the stairs.

Quentin gasped as Hunter's face came into the light, and he jumped to his feet. "What the fuck happened to your face?"

"Nothing."

"Nothing didn't give you a black eye and a scratch across half your face."

Hunter's hair was a mess, and he had dirt on his clothes as well. His jaw tensed. "Fine. I got into a fight, okay? Are you happy now?"

Quentin raced toward Hunter. "No, I'm not happy." He lifted his hand to touch Hunter but quickly remembered to drop it. "What happened? Why did you get in a fight?"

Hunter looked him in the eye. "Let it go, Quentin."

"You know I can't do that. I'm a cop and a sentinel. I can't let you get your ass kicked."

A fire lit behind Hunter's eyes, and he stepped forward. Quentin moved back. The two continued until his back hit the porch railing.

"You think I can't defend myself? You think I'm some pussy who can't fight back? You think because I got hurt last year, I can't take care of myself?" He pointed his finger in Quentin's face. "I'm not some helpless loser."

Quentin knew Hunter was furious. He could see it in the vampire's eyes. He could smell the anger coming off him. Anyone else would be afraid, being backed up the way he had. But Quentin was turned on as fuck.

And Hunter knew it. The heat in his eyes turned from outrage to sexual.

Quentin wasn't sure who grabbed whom. All he knew was that their bodies collided in a fiery kiss.

EIGHT

HUNTER GRABBED on to Quentin's shirt as if he could possibly bring the wolf closer to him. Hunter shoved his tongue into Quentin's mouth. He tasted so good. It had been way too long since he had been near him like this.

Quentin grabbed Hunter's ass, yanking him close, and Quentin's hard cock rubbed against his own.

Hunter groaned. He was afraid he'd come in his pants before they could get to the good stuff.

The good stuff? He was fucking nuts.

There wasn't going to be any good stuff. Quentin had a boyfriend—or someone pretty close to a boyfriend—and he was going to push Hunter away at any second.

But Hunter was going to enjoy the moment before that happened.

Hunter touched the back of Quentin's head and ran his fingers over the wolf's cheeks. He drew his palms down Quentin's chest and over his washboard stomach. Hunter shoved his ass back enough that he could cup Quentin's cock with both hands.

He couldn't believe that thing had been inside him. He had

thought it would hurt. But there had only been a second of pain before Quentin brought him pleasure. He'd read about the prostate gland, and Quentin's dick was the perfect size to hit his.

Hunter moved his hands around to Quentin's butt, so he could rub his own shaft on Quentin's again.

It wasn't fair how much he wanted this wolf.

Quentin fisted Hunter's shirt in his hands, and Hunter braced for being pushed away. But he wasn't prepared for Quentin to flip him around, so his back was to the porch railing.

In a flash, Quentin had Hunter's pants open and his cock in his hand.

Hunter hissed and closed his eyes.

Something about Quentin touching him turned him on like no other.

Hunter had messed around with a couple of other guys in the last year. Even though he was deep in the closet, he wasn't going to fool himself into thinking he could make himself like females. So, he had gone to a couple of bars that he knew would be full of humans and searched for someone who wasn't looking for a commitment.

He'd sucked a few dicks and had his sucked in return, but Quentin's hand felt better than anyone else's mouth ever had.

"Open your eyes," Quentin demanded.

Hunter complied.

Quentin's dark eyes were blazing. "What is it about you?"

Hunter swallowed, but Quentin turned him around before he could answer.

He pulled Hunter back toward his body and stroked his cock. It wasn't long before pre-cum was sliding down the head.

Quentin groaned and squeezed until more leaked out. He swiped it all up on his fingers and pushed Hunter forward. "Hang on to the rail."

Hunter reached up just as Quentin's hand pushed between his ass and spread the pre-cum over his puckered hole. Quentin pushed a finger inside.

"Holy fu—" Hunter was cut off as a second finger went into him. It hurt a little, and Quentin seemed to know.

He reached around to Hunter's dick a few more times, pumping him until he seemed to be satisfied with the amount of pre-cum he'd taken from Hunter's body.

Quentin spread Hunter's cheeks, and Hunter felt Quentin's heavy cock hit him just above his hole. Quentin's had so much pre-cum that it ran down Hunter's leg, and he almost came, knowing that Quentin wanted him that badly.

"Ready?" Quentin asked.

Hunter barely nodded before Quentin pushed inside him.

"Fuck yes," Quentin said.

Hunter lost his breath as he waited for Quentin to bottom out. And when Quentin hit his prostate, he moaned.

Usually, when you remembered something, you put it on some sort of memory pedestal, and when you did it again, it was never as good as it had been the first time.

But this time, it was the opposite.

It was better than he remembered.

Hunter reached back and dug his fingers into Quentin's hip. "Fuck me. Please."

Quentin growled and gripped Hunter as he pulled out and slammed back in. He held himself still for a few seconds before he started pumping his hips.

Hunter had to let go of Quentin and hold on to the rail again before he fell or hit his head on the porch. But that was exactly how he wanted it. Hard and fast.

Trey had taken Hunter to a secret fight club, where he had tried to pound out the turmoil inside him. But the fights earlier tonight had done nothing to take away his pain or the emptiness in his chest.

But in this moment, with Quentin, he could forget about all that.

Quentin's fingers bit into Hunter's sides as the wolf pounded into him with a considerable amount of strength. Hunter knew Quentin was close, and just two seconds later, Quentin exploded inside Hunter.

The knot in Quentin's cock had been put there by Mother Nature to help Quentin get females pregnant, but right now, it filled Hunter fuller than he'd ever been before. The one time they'd done this in the past, Quentin had pulled out and come on Hunter's stomach.

Quentin pulled Hunter to a standing position. As much as he could anyway with Quentin still deep in his ass. Hunter was a few inches taller than Quentin, so he laid his head back against Quentin's forehead.

He was still rock hard, and he wasn't sure what to do about it. He'd never been in this position. He wasn't sure if he should jack off right there, ask for Quentin to do it for him, or leave and take a few minutes in the downstairs bathroom before he went up to bed.

But that was all answered for him when Quentin took Hunter's cock in one hand and shoved his wrist in his face with the other.

"What are—ooh..." Hunter sucked in a breath and gripped Quentin's arm. "What are you doing?"

Quentin stroked his strong fist down Hunter's shaft. "I want you to feed from me while I make you come." His voice was laced with anger.

Hunter lifted his head and shook it.

Sex was one thing, but feeding from Quentin was another, especially during sex. He already had feelings for the guy.

Quentin cursed and pulled his wrist away.

Hunter felt a mix of relief and disappointment.

But Quentin quickly brought his arm back, this time with blood dripping off him.

"What did you do?" Hunter gasped out. The smell of Quentin's blood was intoxicating, and his hunger flared.

"Cut myself with my fangs." He swiped his wrist over Hunter's lip as he kissed his neck. "Now, drink before all my blood goes to waste on the ground."

Hunter only had so much willpower, and he grabbed on to Quentin and pushed his fangs into the wolf.

"Holy shit," Quentin yelled out as his hips thrust forward and he squeezed Hunter harder.

Hunter would like to say that he had stamina, but being surrounded by Quentin turned him into a teenage boy. There was hardly any buildup; he was suddenly just coming.

He let his orgasm wash through him before he licked Quentin's wounds and dropped the shifter's limb.

Quentin's knot had receded, and he withdrew from Hunter. Hunter quickly pulled up his pants.

Not wanting to look at Quentin yet, he used his foot to spread his seed and Quentin's blood around on the grass. He could only hope that no one would smell either of the body fluids when they woke up in the morning.

Hunter finally lifted his head, still not quite sure what to say to Quentin, but it didn't matter. While Hunter had been lost in his own thoughts, Quentin had slipped away.

And Hunter was once again alone.

NINE

RAVEN HAD JUST FINISHED GETTING DRESSED when her phone pinged.

Damien: My office, ten minutes.

Since she was already set to face the day, she headed to the kitchen to pick up something for breakfast before meeting Damien.

She grabbed a bagel, spread on a healthy layer of cream cheese, and went to the alpha's office. Lachlan was already sitting in one of the chairs with his computer open on his lap.

"Morning," Raven greeted them.

"Hey, Raven," Damien said. "We're just waiting for—ah, never mind. Everyone's here."

Raven looked over her shoulder to see Ranulf and Chase walking in behind her. "Hey, guys," she said casually and picked a chair.

She felt better this morning, and the strange attraction she'd noticed toward both men last night seemed to have disappeared. It must have been a weird fluke. One she was all too happy to get rid of.

Damien rubbed his hands together. "So, where are we on the Clifton case? Anything on Chuck Summers?"

Yvette Clifton, a wolf-shifter, had come to Damien when her daughter, Willow, turned up missing. Weeks before, Willow had started acting differently, Yvette told them.

After doing a little investigating, Damien and the other sentinels narrowed in on an after-school program that Willow had been attending. Another girl—human—who had ties to the place had also gone missing. The police wrote her off as a runaway. But the after-school center was the last one to see Willow.

It took about two weeks for Raven to get a volunteer position and start working there. That had been five days ago, and Raven had immediately taken notice of a male volunteer named Chuck Summers. The kids all really appeared to like him, but he seemed to love his position a little too much. He rubbed Raven the wrong way, and she didn't trust him.

"Ranulf and I have taken turns in following him, and he hasn't done anything weird." Chase looked at Ranulf and back at Damien. "In fact, he seems to lead a very boring life. He's single. He visits his mom frequently, and he goes to church. He hasn't made any outside visible contact with any of the kids from the program."

Damien turned his attention to Lachlan.

Lachlan shook his head. "Chuck hasn't made electronic contact with any of the kids either. No texts. No messages on any sites. He doesn't even follow any of them on social media. It's like Chase said. He leads a pretty boring life. Even the porn he looks at is boring."

Ranulf snorted, and Chase burst out laughing. Raven just chuckled to herself as Damien smiled.

"The most exciting thing is, he's been chatting with a woman he met on a dating website, but so far, he's been a gentleman."

Damien seemed to mull this over and looked at Raven.

"I have a shift there this afternoon. I will do some more digging."

Damien nodded. "Just be careful. We don't want anyone thinking you're asking too many questions."

She raised her brow. "I'm always careful."

"Good." Damien stood. "Let me know if you need anything else. Until then, we might have to bring in another volunteer."

Raven got up from her chair as well. "They don't need anyone right now, but if someone quits, I'll let you know."

"Thanks. Good work, guys. Let's do this again tomorrow. Unless Raven finds something." He met her eyes. "Then, you call me right away."

She nodded. "Will do."

☾

When Raven walked into the building where the after-school care took place, she waved to Monica before heading to the break room to put her stuff away.

Monica, a wolf-shifter, was the person in charge at the center, and she had helped Raven learn the ins and outs of the place on the first day. All the kids seemed to love Monica. Raven felt bad for her. She was going to be devastated if she found out someone was kidnapping girls from the center.

"Hey, Raven," Monica said as she walked into the break room.

"Hey, Monica." Raven closed her closet. "Anything you need me to get started on right away?"

Monica looked down at her clipboard. "Can you set up the table in the back of the room?"

"Chairs, too?"

Monica lifted her head. "No, just the table."

"Okay. Will do."

Raven passed by Chuck and nodded her head in greeting but didn't say anything. She didn't like him and didn't want him to think she did.

After setting up the table and sweeping up the floor around it, she headed to the women's restroom. After she flushed the toilet, she was just about to open the door when two girls walked in, and something told Raven to stop.

She didn't know what it was at first until she realized the two girls weren't saying anything to each other. It seemed odd because most females went to the bathroom together, so they could talk.

Raven silently leaned forward, so she could peek through the crack between the door and the stall. She didn't know either of their names. She'd seen them around but not been introduced to them yet. She did know they were both wolf-shifters though.

"Shh," Girl One told Girl Two.

The two girls perked up their ears.

"Okay, I think we're alone," Girl One said.

Thankfully for Raven, half the doors in the old restroom closed on their own, so Raven's stall didn't look out of the ordinary, and the smell of urine and feces overpowered Raven's scent. If these girls were smart, they'd have checked under each door for legs.

"What did you want to tell me?" Girl Two asked, her voice full of excitement.

Girl One made a squeaking sound. "I got asked to go to one of the parties."

The two clasped hands and jumped up and down.

Raven's shoulders sagged. A stupid high school party. She should have known. It wasn't like she was going to crack the missing Willow case from eavesdropping in the girls' restroom, but she couldn't help feeling disappointed.

"Do you think you can get me an invitation, too?"

And now, Raven felt guilty for spying on them.

Girl One bit her lip in hesitation. "I don't know. Monica said you're not ready yet."

Raven's eyes widened at the sound of Monica's name. It seemed odd that a grown woman would be involved in a high school event.

Girl Two crossed her arms across her chest. "I've done everything she's asked of me. I need the money for prom."

Now, the conversation was getting odder, and Raven's heartbeat picked up.

"You haven't done everything. You haven't sent Monica any nudes."

Girl Two lifted a shoulder, looking defeated. "I don't trust them to not get on the internet."

"That's the point, Gin. Monica needs to know she can trust you. If you keep her secret, she'll keep yours."

"I know; I know."

"It's really not that bad. If you can take one of the boys in Monica's office and give him a BJ and let Monica's brother have sex with you, you can take naked pictures of yourself and send them to her."

Raven's hand flew up to cover her mouth as she tried not to make a sound.

"Will you help me?" Girl Two asked.

"You know I will. I want you to come to the party as much as you do. Monica said there's going to be a lot of rich men there, looking to spend their money."

Girl Two squared her shoulders. "I can do this."

"I'll ask my mom if you can come over for dinner, and we'll do it tonight," Girl One said.

"I'm so nervous yet so excited."

"I know what you mean."

Footsteps could be heard out in the hall.

"We'd better go," Girl One said.

"Yeah."

The two left the restroom, and Raven turned her back to the wall and clutched her chest. It sounded like Monica was prostituting these two girls out. And who knew what others. She couldn't figure out how this tied into Willow and the other missing girl, but it had to be connected.

The thought of those two having sex with rich, old guys for money made her stomach hurt.

Before Raven knew it, she was bending over the toilet and puking.

TEN

QUENTIN'S PHONE RANG, and he lifted it off his nightstand to stare at the number.

It was Jeremiah.

He groaned. *Is fucking someone else cheating if you're not exclusive?*

It sure felt like cheating. Especially since Quentin had just brought Jeremiah home to meet everyone.

He rolled onto his back and threw an arm over his face. He should have never brought Jeremiah here.

The ringing from his phone stopped, and he breathed a sigh of relief. Until it started up again.

He couldn't ignore Jeremiah forever.

"Hello?"

"Oh, hey. Did I wake you? It's not even dinnertime yet."

"Really? I'm all messed up."

Jeremiah chuckled. "What time did you go to bed?"

"Around five," Quentin admitted.

"In the morning?" Jeremiah sounded shocked.

"Yeah."

"Isn't that like…" Jeremiah trailed off.

"Around noon, Switzerland time. Yes."

"What were you doing up so late?"

Thinking about Hunter. Waiting for Hunter. Fucking Hunter. Feeding Hunter. Quentin squeezed his eyes shut and rubbed his wrist. *Goddamn it, Hunter, why can't you just stay away from me? Why can't I stay away from you?*

He couldn't tell Jeremiah what he'd been doing. Not over the phone anyway. He deserved to hear it in person. "I don't know. Wasting a lot of time, apparently. I should have gone to bed earlier." Maybe he wouldn't have done the unthinkable then. "My internal clock is all kinds of fucked up now."

Jeremiah laughed. "You'll be back to normal before you know it."

He doubted it. "Let's hope."

"So…"

Quentin could hear the smile in Jeremiah's voice, and he cringed. He knew what was on Jeremiah's mind.

"When are we going to get some time alone together? I miss you, and I'm horny as hell," Jeremiah said in a seductive tone.

He hated being right.

"I miss you, too." Thank God that was true.

Jeremiah chuckled. "But…"

"But I don't know when we'll get to see each other. I'm going to be playing a lot of catch-up. Both here and at work."

"I get it."

The disappointment in Jeremiah's voice made Quentin's chest hurt. And if he was being honest with himself, he could make time for Jeremiah if he really wanted to. He was being chickenshit because he didn't want to tell Jeremiah he'd had sex with someone else.

"You know what?" Quentin said. "What about tomorrow morning? It'll be early, but I think I can squeeze you in."

"Really?"

"I'm on duty tonight for a while, and then I'm going to try

and get some sleep before I have to be at the station tomorrow."

"What time do you need to be at work?"

"Nine. How does seven sound?"

Jeremiah groaned. "That doesn't give us long."

"I know. But it's better than nothing." And he doubted Jeremiah would want to have anything to do with him once he broke the news.

"Okay. Seven it is. My place?"

"Yes, I'll be there."

"I can't wait."

Quentin closed his eyes. "Me either," he lied.

ELEVEN

RAVEN RACED out of the restroom.

"Raven, are you okay?" Monica asked as she passed.

"I'll be right back," she said over her shoulder, and she pushed open the door and sprinted for her car.

Once she had the door shut, she dialed Damien.

"Damien here."

"It's not Chuck Summers that's the problem. It's Monica..." She drew a blank on Monica's last name but then remembered. "Dahl."

She heard Damien's footsteps on the floor through the phone and then a door close.

"She's behind Willow's disappearance?"

"I don't know that yet, but it seems she's running some sort of prostitution thing with the girls at the center. I heard two of them talking in the restroom."

"What did they say?"

Raven covered her mouth. "I don't want to say it out loud. I already threw up once."

She heard Damien moving again, and a door opened as he called out, "Lachlan, get up here. Stat." He put the receiver back to his mouth. "Can you give me the PG version?"

She took a deep breath. "Basically, she makes the girls do things to earn their way. I don't know if it's to prove that they're ready to have sex for money or if it's so she can blackmail them."

"Probably both," Damien said, sounding defeated.

"I don't know if she's responsible for Willow, but it seems like she could be. These two things happening at the same place would be an awfully big coincidence."

"Agreed," Damien said. "I know it's only been a few days, but is there anything you can tell me right now about her?"

Raven thought about what she'd heard. Her focus had been on Chuck, so she hadn't paid too much attention to Monica.

"I know she's single."

Not too long ago, Monica had been talking about men to another volunteer.

"And I can't remember exactly, but it's been some time since she broke up with her last boyfriend. I just happened to overhear a conversation between her and this other volunteer. She said something about how it was hard to meet nice, good-looking guys. But that's all I know."

"Every little bit helps. Listen, Lachlan's here. We're going to start looking into Monica and come up with a game plan now that we know who the target is."

"What do you want me to do until then?"

"Talk to her. I know it will take a while but try to get some info out of her. Maybe lead with the whole single-gal thing. Get her to trust you."

"Got it."

"What time is your shift over?"

"Five thirty, six. Whenever all the kids are gone."

"All right. Talk to you then."

Raven hung up the phone, grabbed her travel toothbrush and toothpaste, left her vehicle, and slowly made her way back to the building. She needed a few seconds to compose herself. She didn't want Monica to wonder why she was suddenly shooting her dirty looks.

Once she was inside, she went to the restroom to brush her teeth and then waited for Monica to approach her.

"Are you okay?"

"Yeah. I threw up earlier, but I feel better now." Undercover 101: stick as close to the truth as possible. Less lies to remember.

"Oh, I hope you're not ill."

Monica actually looked concerned. Raven couldn't tell if she was a good actress or if there was a part of her that meant it.

"I think it was something I ate because I don't feel sick, and my stomach isn't as queasy."

"Good, because we're going to have a lot of kids today."

"Why is that?"

"It's Friday. There are less after-school activities on Friday. I think teachers want to get home just as much as kids do." Monica laughed.

Raven forced herself to look relaxed. "That makes sense."

"Well, we'd better get to work. Let me know if you feel bad again."

Raven smiled. "Will do."

☾

Raven had kept her eye on Monica all afternoon, but she didn't do anything even remotely suspicious. She didn't pull anyone aside. No secret conversations in corners. In fact, she avoided the two girls who had been talking in the restroom. Who Raven had found out were Calli and Virginia.

The place was winding down, and kids were leaving as their parents came to pick them up. Pretty soon, it was only staff left.

Raven wouldn't have another opportunity to speak with Monica until Monday, so she approached the other female.

"So, I hope you don't mind me asking, but I heard you talking in the break room the other day. You're single?"

Monica's eyes narrowed. "I am. Why do you ask?"

Raven was about to say that she was single, too, when the door opened, and Ranulf and Chase walked in.

"Oh my God, who are they?"

Raven's head whipped around. Monica was clearly infatuated with one of the males or maybe both.

But Raven had no idea what they were doing here, so she didn't say anything to avoid saying the wrong thing.

"I call dibs on the brunette." That would be Chase.

Ranulf met Raven's eye and gave her a small nod. She knew what that meant. *Play along.*

When he reached them, he pulled Raven into his arms and kissed her.

Her brain knew it was all part of some elaborate plan, but her body didn't care. She opened her mouth, and Ranulf slipped his tongue inside.

Raven groaned quietly and nudged her pelvis over Ranulf's. He was hard, and she was getting turned on.

Chase cleared his throat. "Will you two get a room already?"

Ranulf pulled away and looked down at Raven with heat she had never seen before. But he quickly looked to Monica as he tucked Raven next to him. "Sorry about that. I haven't seen Raven for a few days." He pointed to his chest. "I'm Ranulf."

"Raven and Ranulf. That's so cute," Monica said.

"And this is Chase," Raven swiftly said before Monica looked too closely at her and Ranulf. "Chase, this is Monica."

Chase took Monica's hand and kissed her knuckles. "Nice to meet you."

Monica chuckled bashfully.

This female could put on a good act.

Ranulf looked down at Raven. "Are you ready for tonight?"

She had no idea what that meant, but she agreed anyway. "Yep. I just need to get changed." She figured that was a safe assumption. Most women wanted to change after work.

Chase grinned. "It's going to be fun."

"Oh," Monica said, "what are you doing tonight?"

"We're going out. Dinner and then a club or two," Chase answered.

"That sounds like entertaining."

And now, she understood what Ranulf and Chase were doing there.

"You wouldn't want to go with, would you?" Chase asked her. He put his hand up to his mouth and pretended to tell a secret. "It would save me from being the third wheel with these two."

Monica beamed. "I'd love to. I can't make dinner, but I can meet you after."

She had taken the bait. Now, they could get her drunk and pump her for information.

"Great," Chase said. "I can't wait."

Raven stifled a laugh. Yeah, Chase couldn't wait...to interrogate her.

TWELVE

AFTER REHEARSING a million speeches in his head, Quentin decided it was time to let it rest. He was just going to have to let his conversation with Jeremiah in the morning play out the way it was supposed to happen.

He pulled himself from bed and poked his head out into the hall. Hunter's door was closed.

Sunset was a few hours away, so most likely, the vampire was still sleeping. One could hope anyway.

Quentin had no idea what to say to Hunter. He'd gone into the house last night without a word. It was selfish and mean of him.

Yet, at the same time, he wasn't the one sending mixed signals.

Hunter couldn't be with him, yet he'd had sex with Quentin. Twice.

Quentin shook his head and walked to the bathroom. He needed to get Hunter out of his brain, or he wasn't going to be a very efficient sentinel.

He entered the dark room, his eyes not adjusted to the lack of light, and ran into someone.

He didn't need to be told who it was. He smelled Hunter. Worse, he smelled himself on the vampire.

"Why the hell didn't you shower this morning?" he asked Hunter, getting in his face. "You smell like me."

"I was tired, and I didn't feel like it."

"What are you going to tell the others if they ask questions?"

Quentin could see now, and he watched Hunter narrow his eyes as his jaw clenched.

"Since when do you care? I thought you were open with your sexuality."

"Obviously, I am. I brought someone home last night. But you're the one who's still in the closet. I would think you wouldn't want them to know what we did."

"Aww…you care about me," Hunter said sarcastically.

Quentin sighed and responded honestly, "Of course I care about you. That hasn't changed."

Hunter tilted his head and smirked. "Do you hate-fuck everyone you care about?"

"Fuck you, asshole."

The corner of Hunter's mouth tilted up. "You already did."

Quentin pushed his forearm into Hunter's throat, knocking the vampire back against the wall. "I've seemed to reserve the hate-fucking for you only. Don't you feel special?"

He could feel Hunter swallow against his flesh as his arousal filled the air. Both of their arousals hit the air.

"Stop it," Quentin said through clenched teeth and pushed his bare chest and dick into Hunter's.

"I can't help it." Hunter's jaw was as tight as Quentin's. "I can feel you." He closed his eyes. "Inside me." He looked at Quentin again. "You need to work on blocking me out if you're going to keep feeding me."

"I shouldn't have given you my vein."

"So, why did you?"

Because Hunter had been hurt and the thought of anyone else feeding him made Quentin want to punch someone. "It won't happen again."

"You're right. It won't. I can't handle all your emotions. You're worse than a female about to go into heat."

"I can't help it that you want me."

Hunter snorted. "Don't flatter yourself. You're the only guy I've fucked. I'm sure once I experiment a little more, I'll forget all about you."

Quentin knew Hunter's words were aimed to piss him off, but all they did was hurt him instead.

Quentin let go of Hunter and stepped back. "Why do you hate me?"

☾

Hunter let his head fall. "I don't hate you." *I hate myself.*

"If that's true, I wouldn't want to see how you treated someone you actually did hate."

Hunter lifted his eyes and blew out a breath. "I'm sorry I'm such a prick."

Quentin put his hands on his hips. "Why are you such an asshole?"

Hunter shrugged. There were a lot of reasons. Because Quentin had left him alone last night. Because he wanted Quentin and couldn't have him. Because, in the end, someone else was going to make Quentin happy. Maybe even that Jeremiah guy.

And didn't that just hurt.

He rubbed his chest.

"Are you okay? Are you injured from last night?"

Hunter dropped his hand. "No. I'm fine." He stepped around Quentin, toward the bathtub. "Can you hit the light?"

Quentin did as he'd asked just as he turned on the water.

"Why were you in the dark anyway?"

"Because I'd just woken up." And Hunter didn't want to have to look at himself in the mirror. He put his fingers inside the seam of his boxers. "I'm going to take that shower now. Are you going to get out or watch?" he asked over his shoulder.

Quentin was staring at Hunter's ass, but the question must have finally gotten through to him. "I'm going."

He moved out into the hall, and that was when Hunter realized they'd been fighting with the door open.

Hunter had no common sense when it came to Quentin. If he did, he would ask Dante if he could move back in with the vampires. Yet he hadn't uttered a word to the Guardian leader.

Hunter pushed his underwear down and got under the spray, wishing he could wash his desire for Quentin off him as easily as he could wash off his scent.

THIRTEEN

RAVEN GLANCED at her phone for what felt like the fifth time and set it on the table in the back of the nightclub. "I don't think she's going to show."

"She'll show," Chase said. "She's got a thing for dark-haired guys."

While Raven had been at the after-school center, Lachlan had been doing some research on Monica. Turned out, all her ex-boyfriends had been dark, and since Raven had overheard her talking about being single, Damien had decided to send in Ranulf and Chase.

Earlier, Raven had been confident that Monica had bought everything they'd been selling, but her doubts were getting stronger by the second. Monica was obviously a very good actress. She could have been playing the three of them right back.

Ranulf put his arm around her. "You need to relax and act like you're having a good time."

"If I knew she was coming, I'd be able to relax a little." She bit her lip. "Maybe if I text her one more time to see if she's coming."

Chase put his hand on her bare leg. "Don't you dare."

Chase's hand was hot on her flesh, and she swallowed. She should not be thinking about how good her fellow sentinel felt.

But Chase pulled away as fast as he'd touched her. "She's here." He stood and held up two fingers, so Monica could see him.

"Game time," Ranulf said and ran his thumb over the back of her bare neck.

She barely held back her shiver from his touch.

What is wrong with me? She was liking both Ranulf's and Chase's touches way too much.

She quickly did some math in her head and realized she hadn't been intimate with anyone in a long time. She was due. Her wolf was due.

Shifters could only go so long without being with someone. They had pack animals in their DNA, and if their animal side didn't get enough physical affection, it started to take over until it got what it wanted.

Raven needed to call up someone after tonight, so she could fix her little problem and concentrate on her job.

Ranulf pulled the spaghetti strap of her dress down her shoulder and kissed her neck. His tongue darted out, and he sucked on her skin.

Raven rubbed her legs together. Ranulf didn't have to go this far to sell the boyfriend-girlfriend thing to Monica.

Monica reached their table, and Chase kissed her on the cheek.

Raven elbowed Ranulf in the chest, and the male lifted his head and smiled. "Hey, Monica. You made it."

She grinned. "Hell yeah, I did. I needed a night out."

Raven relaxed a little now that Monica was there and seemed to be in a good and open mood.

"We were waiting to get drinks until you got here," Chase said. "Can I get you anything?"

"I'll have a Manhattan, please."

Chase looked at Raven and Ranulf. "And what do you two want?"

They each put in their request, and Chase headed to the bar.

"So, how long have you two been together?" Monica asked.

Raven pretended to think about it. "About seven months." In reality, they'd come up with all the answers to these questions before they arrived tonight. "Right, babe?" she asked Ranulf.

He shrugged. "You're better at keeping track of that stuff than me."

Raven looked at Monica and rolled her eyes. "Men."

Monica laughed.

Chase was back before they knew it. It was relatively early in the night, so he hadn't had to wait long at the bar to get drinks. That was one of the reasons the three of them had gone early. They didn't want a ton of people around while they tried to gather intel on the female wolf.

Raven took a sip of her virgin drink and smiled. "Ooh, that's strong."

"Mine is strong, too," Monica said.

Raven just hoped it was strong enough to get Monica tipsy. Hopefully, she'd be more open, the more she drank. It was going to take more than one night to get Monica to trust Raven and tell her what she was doing with the girls, but getting drunk together was an excellent way to start.

The four of them made small talk as the three sentinels took turns in getting rounds.

Ranulf was about to go up again when Monica held up her hand. "Stop," she said in a firm voice.

Ranulf, Chase, and Raven froze.

"What's wrong?" Raven asked.

"You guys have bought all my drinks. It's my turn to get them."

Raven was pretty sure they all breathed a sigh of relief. For a second, she had thought Monica was onto them.

"We asked you to come out with us," Chase said. "It's only fair that we pay."

Monica shook her head. "Nope. I'm getting the alcohol this time."

They couldn't argue too much without tipping her off that something was up.

"Okay," Raven said. "Hurry back."

As Monica rushed off, Raven looked around the table. "It's one drink. We'll be fine."

"I know," Ranulf said. "That little amount of alcohol won't hurt us, but I'm still not comfortable with it."

"Same," Chase said.

"I'll take Monica to the restroom and dump mine out in the sink. You can dump yours out while we're gone."

"Good plan," Chase said. He looked up. "Wow. She's already on her way back." He squinted. "And she's carrying a tray."

Raven looked over. "Shit. She's bringing shots. There's no way we can avoid taking those."

"We'll be fine," Ranulf said. "Especially if we throw out our drinks. One shot won't hurt us."

Raven knew he was right. It took a lot more alcohol to affect them, which was why they had been buying Monica so many rounds with real alcohol while their orders had all been virgin drinks. But something didn't feel right, and it made Raven uneasy.

Monica set the tray down on the table. "I bought shots," she said with a grin.

"You sure did," Raven said.

Monica laughed and pushed a glass in front of each of

them along with their drinks. "I thought we could toast to a new friendship."

There was no getting out of this.

Raven picked up her shot. "To new friends," she said, raising it high.

Chase and Ranulf followed. "To new friends," they repeated.

The four of them raised their shot glasses and clinked them together. Raven brought hers to her lips and swallowed the whole thing down.

FOURTEEN

THE SUN WAS DOWN as Hunter exited his room and headed downstairs. It was time to get out of this stupid house and away from Quentin.

The wolf-shifter alpha, Quentin, Zane, Kendall, and Lachlan were already in the living room along with Payton and Isabelle when Hunter got there. Raven, Chase, and Ranulf hadn't arrived yet.

Damien looked over at him. "Oh, hey, Hunter. I'm going to send Quentin with you tonight since he just got home."

Hunter took a step back, but before he could question Damien, Quentin spoke up, "I don't know, Damien. I think you should send me with someone else. Or I can go on my own. It's not like I've never done this before."

Damien shook his head. "I want to ease you back in. Plus, you have to be at work tomorrow morning, so you can't stay out all night. It's better to put you with someone."

Quentin cleared his throat. "Okay. What about someone else?"

Damien shook his head again. "Chase, Ranulf, and Raven are gone tonight. They're working on something else. Zane is helping the cat-shifters tonight, and Lachlan is doing important research."

Kendall held up her hand. "What about me? I can go with Quentin."

Hunter liked this idea.

And so did Quentin, it seemed, because he said, "Kendall works."

Damien snorted. "Kendall is not going anywhere." He lowered his chin and lifted his brow at her. "She's pregnant, and we don't have enough shifter babies in the world as it is."

Kendall stomped her foot. "This is not fair. And Quentin can protect me."

Damien laughed. "If he's protecting you, then he can't do his job of protecting others."

She crossed her arms over her chest and pursed her lips. "I hate being pregnant."

Payton cleared her throat, and Kendall's eyes widened.

"I'm sorry, Payton." Kendall put her head in her hands. "I'm the worst."

Payton and Damien had tried to get pregnant during her last two heats but hadn't succeeded. It wasn't uncommon from what Hunter understood, but it probably didn't lessen the pain.

Payton walked over and put her arm around Kendall. "You're not the worst. You just need to remember to not put your foot in your mouth," she joked. "Besides, Damien and I are trying again next month, and I have a good feeling about this."

All the males looked at Damien, who cleared his throat. "Baby girl, how about we don't include everyone in our sex life?"

Payton shrugged. "It's not like they're not going to know, Damien, when you're unavailable for a few days."

Damien slapped his hands together. "Anyway, my decision

is final. Quentin, you're riding with Hunter. Zane, you're heading over to the cats. Lachlan, my office, and, Kendall…"

She put her hands on her hips. "You can at least let me help Lachlan or do something around here."

Damien seemed to think about this. "Okay. You can come and help. It doesn't hurt to have more input."

Kendall pumped her fist. "*Yes*." Then, she dropped her arm and looked unimpressed. "This is what my life has come to." She turned and headed out of the room. "I'll meet you in the office."

Quentin looked at Hunter. "I guess we should go then."

"I suppose we should."

They silently walked outside.

"Who's driving?" Quentin asked.

"It's up to you."

"No, you decide." Then, Quentin threw his head back and gave a humorless laugh.

Hunter sighed. "If you want to drive, drive. If you want me to, just say it."

Quentin lowered his chin. "It's not that."

"Then, what is it?"

"Either we're fighting or being overly polite." He stepped close to Hunter. "Can we somehow find a middle ground and be friends?"

Hunter looked away. He didn't want to be friends. But it wasn't Quentin's fault that they couldn't be together. It was his own. He'd never thought it before, but right now, he hated being a vampire.

He sucked in a lungful of air, slowly exhaled, and turned back to Quentin. "Okay."

Quentin raised an eyebrow. "Okay what?"

"Let's try the whole being-friends thing."

Quentin's face lit up in surprise. "Really?"

The wolf's expression made Hunter chuckle even though

he wanted to hang on to his anger. "Yes. I don't want to keep fighting."

"Me either." Quentin held out his hand. "Friends?"

Hunter grabbed it and shook it. "Friends."

The two of them held on a little longer than necessary, but Hunter's common sense kicked in. "First rule of friendship: no extra benefits."

Quentin barked out a laugh. The genuineness of it warmed Hunter's heart. "Good one, Hunter."

Hunter pulled his hand from Quentin's with a smile. "I try. But in all seriousness, we really should avoid touching each other. I'm still a vampire, and you're still…"

"Seeing someone else."

"Yeah, that."

Quentin cocked his head. "Do you really think we can make this work?"

"If I can get run over by a car, I can be friends with you."

Quentin grinned. "I shouldn't laugh because you getting hit wasn't funny, but when you compare the two…well, there is no comparison, is there?"

"Not really." He slapped Quentin on the shoulder. "Come on. Let's get going."

"Okay. And I think that I'd like to drive. I haven't driven in eleven months."

"In that case, why don't we each take our own cars?"

Quentin chuckled. "Did you become a stand-up comedian while I was gone?"

Hunter waved his hand in front of him. "Nah." He was just trying to ignore the slight pang in his heart. He opened the passenger door to Quentin's SUV. "But joking aside, please don't kill me."

Quentin opened his own door. "I'll see what I can do."

FIFTEEN

RAVEN'S PLAN TO dump out their drinks was completed without any complications. She'd managed to pour her drink down the sink while Monica wasn't looking, and when the two females had gotten back to the table, she had seen that Ranulf's and Chase's drinks were empty, too.

"Hey, what do you say we take this little party out onto the dance floor?" Monica said, wiggling her eyebrows.

The three sentinels looked at each other, and Raven shrugged.

Why not? She liked dancing.

Although, as they got up from the table, she realized she was going to have to dirty-dance with Ranulf since he was her fake boyfriend. But she could do this. They were professionals after all.

As they walked out to the floor, Ranulf took her hand in his.

"Are you this affectionate with real girlfriends?"

He always struck her as more of a no-PDA type of guy.

He shrugged.

They found an open spot, and he pulled her into his arms.

"What does that mean?"

"It means, I've never had a girlfriend, so I don't know."

She pulled back to look at his face. "Whaaaaat?"

Ranulf rolled his eyes. "Stop it." He pulled her close again and rubbed his nose against her temple. "I'm not sure if Monica likes Chase."

Since the current song had a fast tempo, Raven walked back, so she could get a better look.

Ranulf was right. Monica was smiling, but she wasn't letting Chase get too close to her.

She could be someone who took things slow. But that seemed like a weird contradiction for someone who pimped out young girls and made them do things in her office.

Monica brought the four of them close. "I'm going to get more drinks."

Chase shook his head. "No, it's my turn."

Monica smiled and waved a finger at him. "I don't think so. It's on me again."

"You know what?" Raven said. "I don't think I'm going to drink any more tonight."

Monica laughed way too hard for something that wasn't funny. "You're not even drunk. And trust me"—she picked up Chase's arm and looked at his watch—"in about ten minutes, you're going to be very grateful I brought you something."

Raven had no idea what Monica meant. "Sure." She stepped back and whispered in Ranulf's ear, "Waste your money then."

He snickered at Raven's comment but was the only one who didn't bother arguing with Monica. "Just let her go. We'll figure something out," he mumbled to Raven.

Raven turned to Monica. "Okay, fine. Bring me another."

Monica grinned. "I'll be back. In the meantime"—she pushed Chase toward Ranulf and Raven until he was at Raven's back—"you can dance with these two."

The she-wolf took off, and Raven was going to suggest they leave the dance floor when one of her favorite songs started playing. It seemed that one shot had hit her system because, suddenly, she was all about getting her groove on. She threw her arms around Ranulf and backed her ass up against Chase.

She didn't know if it was the music, but she was beginning to feel really good. She forgot about Monica and trying to get information out of the female.

She was also starting to get turned on, and so were Ranulf and Chase. She could smell their desire, which was saying something because the club already smelled like a hundred horny people. But it was as if Ranulf's and Chase's scents were going straight to her pussy.

She let her head fall back against Chase, who ran his hands up her abdomen and cupped her breasts. He thumbed her hard nipples while Ranulf glided his hands up the outside of her thighs until he reached the seam of her thong. He gripped her hips and yanked her, so her core was right over his erection.

Raven moaned, and Chase nudged her cheek until she moved her mouth enough, so he could kiss her. She took one of her hands from Ranulf's neck and put it behind Chase's head.

Damn. He was a great kisser.

But then she remembered Ranulf. He'd kissed her that afternoon. She should see who was better. She needed to do a thorough comparison.

She let go of Chase and lifted her head, heading straight for Ranulf's mouth.

Mmm. Just as she remembered. He was a great kisser, too.

☾

Hunter and Quentin got back to the house around one in the morning. Things had been surprisingly civil between them. Hunter had had his doubts that they could stay cordial with one another, but they'd done it.

They were less than five minutes from the house when Quentin's cell rang. He hit the button on his steering wheel to answer without looking at who was calling.

But Hunter saw the name, and he cringed as the vehicle connected.

"Quentin here."

"Hey, babe."

Quentin chuckled and looked at Hunter. *Sorry*, he mouthed with a smile.

Hunter tried to smile back, but it was hard. Just because he'd agreed to be friends didn't mean he was okay with hearing or seeing Quentin's new guy.

"Hey, Jeremiah. You're on speaker, and I'm not alone."

"You're still working?" Jeremiah sounded concerned.

A rush of guilt washed over Hunter. He hadn't been thinking about this guy when he had sex with Quentin. Jeremiah didn't know that Hunter had feelings for Quentin.

Hunter looked out the window.

"Yes, but heading home now," Quentin answered Jeremiah.

"Good. Are we still on for tomorrow morning?"

"Technically, it's this morning."

"If you haven't gone to bed yet, it's tomorrow."

Quentin laughed. "I can get behind that. Talk to you in the morning?"

"Yes."

"Good night."

"Good night, babe."

The call ended, and silence filled the space. Hunter made a note to turn on the radio the next time he was on duty with Quentin.

Quentin cleared his throat. "I'm sorry about that."

Hunter schooled his face and turned away from the window. "It's no problem. We all get phone calls from time to time."

"Yeah, but I'm sure that wasn't fun for you to hear. And I feel bad."

Hunter clenched his jaw. He didn't want Quentin to feel sorry for him. "It's no big deal. Really. You have a special male in your life. If we're going to be friends, I don't want you to have to tiptoe around me."

Quentin looked surprisingly pleased with this. "Thanks, Hunter. Although I don't know if Jeremiah is going to stick around after I tell him I had sex with someone else."

The guilt was back. "You're going to tell him?"

"I can't keep it from him. That's not fair," Quentin said as he turned down their driveway.

Nothing about the situation was fair. To anyone. But Hunter kept that to himself since it was his choice not to come out of the closet.

Quentin pulled into an open spot and parked his SUV. "Thanks again."

Hunter already had the door open and was out of the vehicle. "No problem." He shut the door, careful not to slam it and give himself away.

Quentin got out of the driver's seat as Hunter walked around to his own SUV and hit unlock on his key fob.

"Hunter?" Quentin's brow was furrowed.

Hunter opened his vehicle's door. "Yeah?"

"Where are you—" He cut himself off and changed his question. "Are we okay?"

Hunter forced the biggest smile he could on his face. "We're good."

"Okay. See you tomorrow."

"Tomorrow." Hunter got in and shut his door before he had to say anything else to Quentin.

He pulled out his phone and hit Trey's number.

Hunter: Where's everyone meeting tonight?

Trey: You got a taste for fighting, and you want more, huh?

Hunter: Something like that.

Trey: I'll send you the coordinates.

Hunter drove to where the fights were taking place that night as fast as he could without getting pulled over for speeding.

As he pulled into the large field, he noticed that it was a bigger turnout than the night before, which was understandable since it was Friday.

Hunter got out of his car and walked around the circle of people cheering for the two individuals who were fighting in the middle. Last night, he'd learned they were a mixture of onlookers and other fighters.

If they wanted to keep this whole event secret, Hunter thought they needed to stop inviting people, but he wasn't in charge.

Hunter found Trey up front with a couple of other males. One was skinny and counting money, and another was huge and standing with his arms crossed over his chest and a scowl on his face.

"Hey, Hunter," Trey called out when he spotted him.

"Hey," Hunter said back.

"Hunter, this is Wayne."

Wayne paused in his money-counting for all of two seconds to nod a greeting to Hunter.

"And this is Tank," Trey said, putting his hand on the big guy's shoulder.

Tank narrowed his eyes at Trey's hand and growled.

Trey yanked his arm away and chuckled nervously. "Wayne and Tank are brothers and in charge of this whole thing."

Wayne sighed and looked up. "Now, why the fuck would you say that?"

"Don't worry about it, man. Hunter's good people. He's the one who brought in so much money last night."

"Trey's right," Hunter said. "I couldn't give two shits who's in charge. I just came to fight."

He should care. He should be telling Damien and Dante about this place, but he had followed the rules his whole life, and look where that had gotten him. Alone.

And it wasn't like they were killing anyone. The fights were stopped before they reached that point. What Dante and Damien didn't know wouldn't hurt them.

Tank put his hand on the back of Hunter's neck, and while he noticed how large it was, he wasn't going to be intimidated.

"You fight next," Tank commanded.

Hunter shrugged off Tank's hand. He peeled off his leather jacket and shirt and threw them behind him on the ground. He rubbed his hands together. "I'm ready."

"Jess, get your ass in the middle. You're fighting…"

"Hunter."

Tank nodded toward the center of people. "Well then, get the fuck in there."

Jess smirked at Hunter and bared his fangs. That was all the invitation Hunter needed to hit the other vampire. He walked up to Jess and punched the male in the face. As his opponent fell back and tried to stay on his feet, a calm began to settle over Hunter.

By the end of the fight, he was smiling again.

SIXTEEN

THE NEXT MORNING, Quentin knocked on Jeremiah's door and stood back as he waited for him to answer.

He had been feeling pretty good about talking to Jeremiah, but now that he was here, his nerves were kicking in. He didn't care who someone was. No one wanted a conversation like the one he was about to have.

The door swung open, and Jeremiah stood there in jeans, wet hair, and a smile.

Damn it. He looked good.

Quentin stepped closer, and Jeremiah clutched the front of his shirt and pulled him inside. He pushed Quentin up against the wall and kissed him.

Quentin melted into Jeremiah, remembering their time together in Switzerland. They'd been so happy.

Even if Jeremiah wasn't as good of a kisser as Hunter.

If there were a soundtrack to his life, this was when the sound of a record scratching would stop the music playing in the background.

Quentin put his hands on Jeremiah's arms and gently set him back a foot.

Jeremiah furrowed his brow. "What's wrong?"

"We need to talk."

"Uh-oh," Jeremiah joked, but he lost his smile when he saw that Quentin wasn't smiling back.

"Can we sit down?" Quentin asked.

"Yeah, yeah. Come in." Jeremiah led them to the living room.

They both sat on the couch, but Quentin made sure to keep some distance between the two of them.

"What I'm about to tell you is not easy."

"You're breaking it off with me?" Jeremiah guessed. "Seems odd since I just met your family and friends…"

Quentin shook his head. "No, but after I talk to you, you might want to break things off with me."

Jeremiah rubbed his hands on his jeans. "Okay. Hit me with it."

"There's this guy I have a past with. I thought it was completely over, but I saw him again the night of my welcome-home party." Quentin took a deep breath and slowly exhaled. "I didn't intend for it to happen, but—"

Jeremiah held up his hand. "If you're going to say you had sex, I don't want to hear any more."

A pregnant pause filled the space between them, and Quentin found that he couldn't be quiet. "I know words mean crap, but I'm really sorry."

"Wow." Jeremiah chuckled in a way that sounded like he couldn't believe the situation was real. "I didn't realize how much I wanted—no, expected—you to say you didn't have sex." He stood from his couch and started pacing.

"I can't tell you that. I'm sorry."

Jeremiah stopped in front of Quentin. "Who is this guy?"

Quentin winced. He didn't want to tell Jeremiah that the guy he'd had sex with was Hunter because Jeremiah and Hunter were bound to run into each other. If Jeremiah didn't break things off with him and things progressed to being exclusive, Quentin would tell him. By then, he'd know who Hunter was as an individual and not as the other guy.

"You're not going to tell me, are you?"

"No. The other male has nothing to do with you and me, and I don't want him caught in any cross fire."

Jeremiah took a step back. "What the hell, Quentin? Do you think I'm going to hunt this guy down?"

Quentin bit his cheek at Jeremiah's use of the word *hunt*. He could hunt down *Hunter*.

Don't laugh. Don't laugh. This is not a joke.

He must be stressed if he was laughing at stupid shit.

"I don't think that about you." One thing Quentin liked about Jeremiah was that he was a beta male. Living with a bunch of alphas could get old sometimes. It was nice to be around someone who didn't always exert his dominance. "It's just better if you don't know."

Jeremiah threw his hands in the air. "I don't know what to do here, Quentin. I know we decided to take things slow until we were both home for a few weeks. Is this why you didn't want to take the next step? Because you knew you'd see this guy again and things would happen between the two of you?"

Quentin jumped up. "No. No way. Things were over for us since before I went to Europe."

"Then, why did you two hook up the other night?"

Quentin sighed. "I know you want a nice, simple answer, but I don't have that for you. Things have been complicated between us, even before it was over. I guess not seeing each other for almost a year brought up a lot of feelings."

Jeremiah looked down at his hands. "Do you love him?"

Quentin had to really think about this one.

Jeremiah laughed but looked like he wanted to cry. "Oh God, you do."

Quentin put his hands up. "No. I didn't answer right away

because I wanted to sincerely consider the question. I didn't want to rush in and say no. I wanted to give you an honest answer."

"And that answer is?"

"No, I don't love him. I care about him, and I think I could have loved him if he'd given us a chance. But it never got that far." He stepped closer to Jeremiah. "And you're the one I want to be with."

Jeremiah turned his head away, but Quentin caught the small smile. He looked back at Quentin. "I need to think about things. I know we're not technically boyfriend and boyfriend, but I'm still hurt."

"I know. I really regret that."

"And yet…"

"And yet what?" Quentin asked.

"Never mind. Just give me a little while to think about things, okay? I need some time. I'll let you know where we stand in a few days."

Quentin nodded. "Okay. I understand." He pointed to the door. "I'd better get going then. First day back at work and all."

"Yeah. I'll walk you out."

The two of them silently made their way to Jeremiah's front door. When they reached it, Jeremiah put his hand on the knob but didn't open it.

"You know, when you came over this morning, I thought I'd give you a tour of my place…ending in my bedroom."

Quentin winced. "Fuck. I'm such a shit."

"I didn't say it to make you feel guilty. It's only that life can change in an instant."

"I'm sorry. Again."

Jeremiah smiled. "I know."

Quentin kissed the other male on the cheek. "Let me know when you want to talk again. I'll be ready."

Jeremiah opened the door. "'Kay."

Quentin walked out to his car, feeling relief from telling Jeremiah what had happened yet also like the worst person in the world.

He turned to look at Jeremiah one more time, but the door was already closed.

SEVENTEEN

DAMIEN WALKED INTO THE KITCHEN, staring at his phone. "We have a problem."

Kendall popped a piece of fruit in her mouth. "What's wrong?" She glanced at Lachlan, but he shook his head.

"I don't think Raven, Chase, and Ranulf came home last night."

"What?" Kendall said.

"Yeah. I checked their rooms after they didn't answer, and their scents are old. And now, none of them are answering their phones."

Lachlan got up from the table. "I'll go grab my computer and see if we can ping their phones to find them."

Kendall chewed on her lip in worry. "Did you hear from them at all last night?"

"Not a word," Damien said.

"Shit."

"My thoughts exactly."

Lachlan was back a few seconds later, and Kendall had to hold herself back from yelling at him to hurry up and turn on his computer. It felt like it was taking forever.

"Computer's up," Lachlan said, and he began typing away. After another minute or so that felt like hours, he said, "Okay, good news. All their phones are in the same location."

"How is that good news?" Kendall cried out. "That only means they've all been kidnapped by the same person. They're probably being tortured for information. Oh my God, they're going to die."

Lachlan raised an eyebrow and stared at her like she'd delivered her baby right there on the kitchen floor. "If you'd let me finish, I would have told you that they're at Ranulf and Chase's off-duty apartment."

Kendall slapped a hand to her chest and breathed the biggest sigh of relief. "Oh, thank God."

"Unless someone followed them home and tied them up there."

Kendall shot a dirty look in Lachlan's direction.

"Lachlan," Damien scolded.

He threw his hands up. "It was a joke. They left the club a little after midnight and went straight to the apartment. They didn't make any unusual turns, like someone was following them, and they haven't gone anywhere else. They're probably all sleeping."

Kendall stood and faced Damien. "Permission to go there, please?"

She could see Damien was hesitant.

"It does seem like they're fine and not in any trouble."

Kendall folded her hands and lifted them under her chin. "I'm not above begging."

Damien thought about it for a few more seconds. "Okay, I'll let you go."

"Thank you."

"But I'm going to have Lachlan monitor your phone the whole time."

Kendall nodded. "No problem."

"And if you suspect any trouble—any trouble, Kendall, I mean it—you call me."

"I promise."

Damien walked over to the wall where the key rack was and picked up a set. He came back and put them in Kendall's hand. "Here's the spare set to the apartment. Don't lose these."

"I won't." Kendall tried to pull her hand away, but Damien wouldn't let her. "I'll be fine, Damien."

He rolled his eyes and let go of her. "Okay. Get out of here before I change my mind."

Kendall didn't need to be told twice.

It was the lamest mission she'd gone on as far as she could remember, but she didn't care. She was excited to help out.

And even though she told herself that her friends were fine, she was honestly a tiny bit worried.

☾

Raven was in a boat that wouldn't stop rocking. "Oh…make it stop." She was going to throw up.

"Raven, get up."

She popped one eye open and saw Kendall staring down at her from the end of the bed. "What the hell is going on?"

Kendall shrugged. "I was hoping you could tell me that. You look like shit."

Raven slowly sat up and looked to each side of her.

She'd been sleeping in between Chase and Ranulf.

Oh shit. She hadn't…

She looked at herself to see she was wearing an oversize T-shirt and a pair of boxers. So, while she was currently dressed, she had changed at some point.

She clapped a hand over her crotch. She wasn't sore at all. And she was almost certain that if she'd had sex with both Ranulf and Chase, she would have felt it this morning.

She picked up the single sheet and saw that both of them were wearing boxers, too.

She let her head fall back against the headboard as Kendall snorted.

"Ouch." She rubbed the bump she'd just given herself.

"If it helps, it doesn't smell like sex in here at all." Kendall lifted her nose. "Yep. No sex. It does smell like alcohol though. Did you shoot your drinks directly into your veins?"

"Ha-ha."

"Seriously, I thought the three of you weren't going to drink."

"Me, too." Raven closed her eyes, but she only got flashes of what had happened last night.

She reached out and started shaking both Chase and Ranulf awake.

Both of them groaned, and Kendall kicked the bed a couple of times.

"Did you kick the bed to wake me up?" Raven asked.

"Yep. And it worked. Kind of. I was trying to wake all three of you."

"That would explain the moving boat."

"Huh?"

"I thought I was on a moving boat. Turns out, it was you." Raven slapped her hands down, open palms, on both of the guys. She hit Ranulf in the middle of his back and Chase on his stomach.

Both scrambled up.

"About fricking time," Kendall said.

"What the fuck?" Chase said, rubbing his abdomen. "What the hell did you do that for?"

"You wouldn't wake up."

Ranulf was sitting on the side of the bed, scowling over his shoulder at her with a big red handprint on his back.

"You can stop giving me dirty looks. I tried to be nice. You wouldn't get up either." Raven scooted to the side next to Ranulf and stood.

She immediately saw stars and fell back. Ranulf caught her and set her on his lap.

"You okay?" he asked.

She laid her head on his shoulder. "Yeah. Just got dizzy there for a sec." She inhaled and exhaled and stood again.

"You okay?" Kendall asked.

"I'm good." Raven turned around. "What happened last night?"

Chase rubbed his hand down his face. "I'm not sure. I remember we were dancing…and Monica said she was going to get us drinks."

"That's right," Raven said. "And then—" She clapped her hand over her mouth as her eyes widened.

"What? What happened?" Kendall demanded.

Raven put her head in her hands and adamantly shook it back and forth. "I'm too embarrassed."

"Now, you have to tell me. You know that, right?"

Raven lifted her head to see Chase grinning.

"She made out with Ranulf and me."

Ranulf looked over his shoulder at Chase and then up at Raven with a smirk on his face.

"I hate you both," Raven said.

"What happened next?"

"Someone yelled at us to get a room," Ranulf said.

"Which is saying something for a nightclub," Chase added.

Raven snapped her fingers. "That's right." Thank God someone had interrupted them. "Then, we went to find Monica."

"Yeah, and we couldn't find her," Chase said.

"Correct me if I'm wrong, but I thought you guys weren't drinking last night," Kendall repeated as she put a hand on her hip. "This doesn't seem like you three."

"That's because I think we were drugged," Raven said. "I'm pretty sure Monica roofied us."

EIGHTEEN

QUENTIN'S first day back at work had gone well. At least, the work part did. He had trouble staying off his phone. He'd kept thinking Jeremiah would text him even though he knew it would most likely take more than a day.

When he got home that evening, he was surprised at how tired he was. Taking so much time off had turned him into a wimp. He hoped his body would catch up to how he had been, but tonight, he was glad he would get to go to sleep before he had to be back at the precinct tomorrow.

When he walked into the house, the air was heavy, and he could tell that something was going on.

Damien, Kendall, Raven, Chase, Ranulf, and Payton were sitting in the living room.

"Hey, what's going on?" Quentin asked.

Damien sighed. "We're discussing what Raven's next step should be."

Quentin leaned against the wall. "What happened?"

Damien filled him in on Raven's work at the after-school program, the volunteer there, and about her night out with Chase and Ranulf.

"Jesus," Quentin said. "Were you for sure drugged?"

"We went to the infirmary and had our blood taken. The results were inconclusive," Raven answered.

"That doesn't surprise me. Rapists are constantly making new roofies at home with different ingredients. It's hard for lab tests to keep up." Roofies were something he was all too familiar with when it came to his job. He didn't investigate those crimes as an officer, but he'd been the first to respond to many of those kinds of calls. "What are you going to do about Monica? When will you see her again?"

"I'm supposed to go in on Monday. If I accuse her of drugging us, I might as well give up on figuring out what happened to Willow. But won't she think it's weird if I don't ask her something? I mean, she disappeared on us."

"Do you think she drugged you because she's onto you?" Quentin looked at Ranulf and Chase, too, since they had all been there last night. "Or because she thought it would be fun?" He'd seen more than one person slip something to a friend without them knowing, so it was possible Monica had done the same thing. Pretty ballsy to do with people she hadn't gone out with before though.

The three thought about it, and Chase spoke up first, "I don't think so. Anything's possible, but I don't think we gave her any reason to suspect us. In fact, I thought we were having fun."

"There's only one way to find out. Raven, send Monica a text. Something like, *Hey, girl. I hope you made it home safely last night. Sorry I haven't texted all day. I've been exhausted. Bummer we lost you last night. I think we had too much to drink.* Throw in an *LOL* or a smiley face. Then add, *Chase asked me if I could give you his number, but I wanted to check with you first to make sure it's okay.* Her response should give you enough clues."

"Wow, Quentin. That's amazing," Kendall said.

Quentin chuckled. "Not really. I'm sure one of you would have come up with something."

Damien snorted. "I doubt it. We've been sitting here for a while, and we couldn't come to an agreement."

Quentin pushed himself off the wall and headed for his bedroom. He slapped Damien on the back. "Then, maybe I should be the alpha."

Damien growled, "Over my dead body."

Quentin laughed. "I was joking. You couldn't pay me to be alpha."

"Hey, it's not that bad."

"Whatever you say…boss," Quentin said as he disappeared from their sight and went upstairs.

When he got to his room, he sat down on his bed and flopped back. He groaned as his muscles relaxed.

It wasn't even eight at night, but he was beat. Once he got up enough energy, he was going to take a shower, get something to eat, and go to bed. He didn't even care if it made him look like a pussy.

As he yawned, he realized he must be getting old. Soon, he'd be having dinner at three in the afternoon and going for coffee with his friends every morning.

☾

"Quentin, it worked. Oh, sorry. I didn't know you were sleeping."

Quentin lifted his head off the bed to see Raven standing in his doorway. "No, it's fine." He slowly sat up. "I didn't mean to fall asleep. I'm glad you woke me."

"I guess you're welcome then."

"So, what did she say?"

Raven looked at her phone. "She said she ran into some

friends, and by the time she made it out to the dance floor, we were gone."

"Do you believe her?"

Raven shrugged.

"That part doesn't matter anyway. The point is, you have an open line of communication with her to find out more stuff."

"Exactly."

Quentin grinned. "What did she say about Chase?"

Raven wrinkled her nose. "That part she said no to. She doesn't think she and Chase are into each other that much."

"I guess Chase isn't a very good actor."

She repeatedly tapped her phone against her palm in thought. "But now, it means, I'm on my own. We can't go out on double dates if she doesn't like Chase."

"You could always try to bring Chase in as a client for her."

Her phone stilled as her mouth opened, and her eyes widened. "You're so smart, Quentin. That's a great idea."

"It's nothing."

"We should have done that before. I could have tried to get her to recruit me."

Quentin frowned. "Doesn't she go after high school girls? You're not exactly youn—"

Raven's hand shot up. "Not another word."

Quentin chuckled. "I only meant that you're intelligent. You have a job. You're not desperate for money, nor are you easily controlled."

"If that's what you were going to say from the beginning, then I completely agree."

"Just take it one step at a time. Don't plan too far ahead because you're just going to keep having to switch things up."

"Good advice. But I'll let you get back to sleep."

"Thanks."

Raven walked away, and Quentin looked at his clock. Less than an hour had passed, but now, he wasn't tired. He could offer to go on duty again that night, but he wasn't sure how long his nap would last him. And he needed to be at work again the next day.

Quentin grabbed a clean long-sleeved T-shirt and boxers from his dresser and went to the bathroom to brush his teeth and take a shower. He was in and out in less than ten minutes.

He hung up his towel, trying to decide what he was going to do for the night, and he briefly wondered if Hunter was on duty or if he was off.

Things the night before had gone great. He and Hunter hadn't fought once, and he thought their friends idea might work. Hunter had gotten quiet after Jeremiah called, but Quentin was trying to not feel bad about that.

It wasn't Quentin's fault that Hunter was in the closet or that the guy wanted to stay there.

Quentin wasn't going to be alone his whole life just so Hunter wouldn't have to be hurt.

It still felt shitty though.

Quentin left the bathroom and was going to stop by to say hi to Hunter when the vampire walked out of his own bedroom.

Hunter stalled when he saw Quentin. "Hey."

"Hey yourself. You working tonight?"

"No."

Quentin scanned Hunter. "You look like you're going out."

"Oh. Yeah, I am. Just not on duty, is all."

Quentin smiled. "Why don't I come with you? I'm not on duty either."

Hunter's lips pursed. "I don't think that's a good idea."

"Why not?" Quentin wasn't getting a good feeling about the situation.

"It just isn't."

"Is it for vampires only?"

"No."

"Then, why can't I come?"

Hunter sighed. "Because you can't, okay? You're not invited. Please, stop pushing." He squeezed past Quentin, obviously done with the conversation.

But as Hunter passed him, Quentin saw fresh bruises on the back of Hunter's jaw, under his ear, and on his cheekbone.

He knew that Hunter wasn't going to tell him where they'd come from, so Quentin raced to his room. He threw on jeans, socks, and shoes, and then he ran outside to his SUV.

NINETEEN

AS QUENTIN GOT in and started up his vehicle to follow Hunter, he took deep, calming breaths. Quentin didn't know how to block his emotions like vampires did, and if Hunter figured out that he was being followed, he would most likely abandon his destination.

Quentin needed to be careful.

Putting himself into cop mode helped him. When he was at work, he couldn't let his emotions control him, or he wouldn't be able to do his job.

As they drove, the houses got farther apart, and streetlights disappeared. It would be harder for him to follow Hunter without being spotted, and he hoped Hunter got to his stop soon.

About five minutes later, Hunter pulled into a long driveway of a small, slightly run-down house. Quentin drove past, but as soon as he was around the corner, he turned around in case Hunter had been watching him.

He came back around just in time to see Hunter pull around the back of the house, and Quentin sighed with relief.

Part of him had been worried that Hunter had figured out

he was being tailed and pulled into a random house, so he could turn around and escape.

Quentin pulled to the side of the road and watched the house. It was dark, and even though Hunter was there, no lights came on. When another car drove up and went around to the back of the house, he knew it was time to investigate.

Not wanting an officer or deputy from the county to stop to inspect his vehicle, he started his car and drove down to a church he'd seen about a quarter mile back. He parked in the shadows as much as possible before exiting his vehicle.

He popped his trunk and stripped off his clothes. He threw them in the trunk, shut it, and shifted into his wolf.

He ran the quarter of the mile back to the house in no time. It was easy when he didn't have to stay on the road. He just had to make sure he didn't startle any homeowners who might call animal control. Or worse, pull out their guns and shoot him.

As he got closer to the house, he could hear lots of noise from what had to be a large group of individuals. All shifters and vampires from what he could smell. They were in a huge circle, cheering and booing as their attention was on something in front of them.

As Quentin neared them, he stayed out of the light as much as possible, so no one would see him as he tried to locate Hunter.

He found the vampire when there was an opening in the ring of people. He stood there without a shirt, nodding at what the guy was saying next to him.

It was at this time Quentin could see what was going on in the center of the circle. Two individuals were fighting.

What the hell?

Hunter's back straightened, and Quentin immediately calmed his thoughts. It didn't stop Hunter from looking around. Thankfully, Quentin was able to get behind a tree. He had to stand on his hind legs, but it worked.

He stayed hidden until he felt his heartbeat slow. Only then did he feel it was safe enough for Hunter to not be looking for him.

Quentin came around the tree just as Hunter went into the ring.

Forgetting all about staying out of sight, he moved forward on autopilot as he held his breath. This would explain why Hunter had bruises.

Another male stepped up against Hunter. The two bumped fists before someone yelled, "Fight."

Hunter took a swing and missed. The other guy did the same. While the two danced around each other, Quentin got more worried by the minute.

"What the fuck?" Quentin heard from behind him, but it was too late.

Someone wrapped something around his neck and pulled.

A skinny wolf-shifter grinned down at him. "Try and escape now, asshole."

Quentin lunged for the guy but was knocked onto his back before he even made contact, and he yelped as his ribs hit the ground hard.

☾

Quentin's in trouble.

Hunter turned and looked in the direction where he felt Quentin through his blood. The wolf-shifter had to be close; otherwise, Hunter wouldn't have sensed him.

Whack.

Hunter was so concerned about Quentin that he'd forgotten he was fighting, earning him a right hook across the face.

Hunter fell on the ground and rolled out of the way as his opponent tried to kick him.

He didn't have time to fight, so he jumped to his feet and punched his rival in the face, in the gut, and in the face again. Hunter lifted his leg and gently pushed the guy back until he fell on his ass.

The group around him cheered, but he didn't care. He needed to find Quentin.

He noticed that Wayne and Tank weren't standing in their usual spots, so he jogged over to where they usually kept watch. Once he was around the back of the crowd of people blocking his view, he saw the brothers wrestling a wolf on the ground.

"Stop," Hunter yelled.

Wayne and Tank looked up.

"I know him."

Wayne stepped back, but Tank kept his foot on Quentin's body and a silver chain around Quentin's neck.

"You know this guy?" Wayne asked.

"Yes."

Wayne narrowed his eyes. "We found him sneaking around." He came closer to Hunter. "You're one of our best fighters, but if you're having others investigate us, I will kick you out of here."

Hunter shook his head. "No. He's not investigating. Not you anyway. I'm pretty sure he followed me to investigate what I was doing."

Wayne nodded at Tank, and Tank let Quentin up.

Quentin immediately shifted into his human form.

"This true?" Wayne asked Quentin.

"Yes. I'm not here for you. I'm here for him," he said, pointing to Hunter.

"Put them in the van," Wayne said to his brother. "We need to look into this. I don't know why a wolf-shifter would be looking after a vampire. I don't trust them."

Hunter wanted to take Quentin out of there and go home, but he knew the smart thing would be not to fight. "Can I get my shirt, please?"

Wayne nodded, and Hunter picked up his shirt and threw it at the naked wolf-shifter.

Quentin was shorter than Hunter, but he was bigger through the shoulders and chest, and Hunter's T-shirt stretched across his pecs.

By now, the crowd was watching the exchange, and Wayne noticed. "Mind your business." To Tank, he said, "Get them out of here."

Tank grabbed Quentin and Hunter by the arms and dragged them through the maze of cars until they got to an old VW van. Tank opened the side and dug around in a plastic bag. He pulled out a pair of sweatpants and threw them at Quentin, who hastily put them on. He turned to Hunter and held out his hand. "Phone."

"I don't have one."

Tank huffed and started patting Hunter down. When he found Hunter's keys, he used the key fob to find his SUV. "Stay here."

"Where are we going to go? You have my keys," Hunter pointed out.

"Just keep your ass here."

Tank went and searched around Hunter's vehicle, but he came back with nothing.

Hunter smiled sweetly and held out his hand. "Told ya."

Tank put Hunter's keys in his pocket and pushed Hunter into the van. "I'm not that stupid. I'm keeping the keys for now." He looked at Quentin. "What are you waiting for? Get in."

Quentin clenched his jaw but didn't put up a fight. He got in beside Hunter, and their eyes met right before the door was slammed closed and the overhead light went out.

TWENTY

"WHAT THE FUCK are you doing here?" Hunter hissed at Quentin.

Quentin sighed. "Look, we can talk about this later, but right now, we don't have time. They're going to come back and start asking questions. Our answers need to match."

Quentin's eyes adjusted enough to see Hunter cross his arms over his chest.

"I'll tell them you're my stalker and that you're obsessed with me."

"You wish."

"No, you do."

Quentin ran his hand over his face. "Again, we can talk about this later. What they're doing is illegal. We can't let them find out that you're a Guardian and that I'm a sentinel. And a cop. I'm not sure which one would be worse."

"They're not going to find out. These guys don't exactly run a stand-up operation here."

"We can't risk it. When it comes to criminals, one can never be too careful."

"*When it comes to criminals, one can never be too careful,*" Hunter mocked him in a hoity-toity voice.

"I was worried about you." Quentin groaned in frustration. "I know you're mad at me, and you can yell or make fun of me all you want. After. We're. Safe."

Hunter turned away. "*Fine*. What do you want me to say?"

"As much as we can about the truth. We're friends. I was worried about you, and I followed you here."

Hunter snorted. "That's your big backstory? I'm so glad we stopped fighting so that you could lay all that out." He tapped the side of his head. "I don't know if I'll remember all that."

Pissed now, Quentin got in Hunter's face. "We also shouldn't mention that we've been lovers in the past." He smirked. "Not that I have to worry about that with you, but I thought I'd make sure you knew I wasn't going to say anything either."

Hunter shoved Quentin away. "Fuck you."

Quentin ground his teeth together before he said something snotty back, like, *Been there, done that, got the T-shirt.* "Look, right now, our job is to stay alive. No matter how angry you are, you don't want to see me dead, do you?"

Hunter didn't respond.

Quentin just stared at him.

"Ugh. I don't want you dead, okay? Happy now?"

"No. I'll be happy when we're driving away from here."

The two sat in silence for a few minutes.

Surprisingly, it was Hunter who spoke first, "What do you think they'll do with us?"

"I don't know." Sometimes, it seemed like most criminals were the same, but there were always the ones who surprised you.

The crunch of footsteps outside caught their attention, and they both froze.

The van door slid open, and Quentin winced at the over-head light.

"What are your names?" Skinny Guy asked.

Huge Guy was standing next to him with a phone in his hand and his finger hovering over the screen.

"You already know I'm Hunter. This is Quentin."

"Last names."

Before Hunter could answer, Quentin jumped in. "Mine is Esmund."

He sensed Hunter was going to look at him for using Hunter's last name, so he pinched him in the leg.

Skinny Guy looked at Huge Guy. "Search for Quentin Esmund."

Huge Guy shook his head. "I found a couple of people with the name, but nothing about either of them stands out."

Skinny Guy looked at Hunter. "And yours?"

Quentin prayed that Hunter had caught on to not giving their own names.

Hunter cleared his throat. "Rawling."

Quentin had to stop himself from looking at Hunter. The only reason Quentin had used Hunter's last name was so that Hunter would not use it himself. There was no way a vampire and a shifter were related. Not full-blooded ones anyway.

He hadn't expected Hunter to use his last name, and it made him feel all funny inside. Which it shouldn't have. He was sure that Hunter had used it to keep things simple and less confusing if it came up again.

"Nothing on Hunter Rawling either," Huge Guy said.

Quentin hadn't even been paying attention to the two criminals in front of them because he was lost in thought. He needed to get his head together. Now was not the time to imagine being married to Hunter and Hunter taking his last name.

"Are we free to go now?" Quentin asked.

Skinny Guy grinned, and Quentin had a feeling he wasn't going to like what came out of the guy's mouth. "Just one thing first."

"I'm not killing anyone," Quentin joked.

Skinny Guy laughed a lot harder than Quentin had thought he would. "No killing. You're going to fight."

"Excuse me?" Quentin said as Hunter declared, "No way."

"You look like you work out," Skinny Guy said. "You fight, and we'll let both of you go."

Quentin shrugged. "Sure. Why not?"

Hunter put his hand on Quentin's forearm. "No."

Quentin shook him off. "Not so fun when the shoe is on the other foot, is it?" He stood and hopped out of the van. "I'm ready."

Skinny Guy rubbed his hands together. "This is the kind of cooperation I was hoping for. Come on. I have the perfect opponent for you."

Skinny Guy and Huge Guy walked on ahead, and Hunter jumped out of the van behind him.

"You don't have to do this."

"Yes, I do. This is a test, and if I don't do it, we fail."

"I don't want you to get hurt."

Quentin shrugged. "Shit happens."

He stepped away and followed the two criminals back to the fighting ring. They had already started making an announcement that he was fighting.

Skinny Guy motioned him into the middle of the circle.

"I have a question before we fight," Quentin shouted over the noise of the crowd.

"What's that?"

"What's your name?"

Skinny Guy laughed. "I'm Wayne. And the big guy is Tank, my brother."

Quentin filed that info away for later. Right now, he held

out his hand. "Nice to meet you, Wayne. Under the circumstances."

Wayne shook his hand. "Same to you. You fight good tonight, you're welcome back anytime." Wayne took a step back and shouted, "Are you ready to see who Quentin is going to fight?"

The horde of onlookers cheered.

"He's going to fight…" Wayne held out his pointer finger and began turning in a circle, going past individuals who had their hands raised. He spun around several times before stopping at his selection, his grin back. "Hunter."

Quentin was fucked. Hunter was so mad at him that there might be a killing tonight after all. Hunter might very well beat him to death.

TWENTY-ONE

"*OW.* THAT HURT," Quentin yelled at Hunter.

Hunter lowered the ice pack and sighed. "Hold still and quit being a baby."

Quentin pulled the ice pack out of Hunter's hand and threw it at him. "I'm not being a baby. You fucking sucker-punched me."

Hunter looked at Quentin's open bedroom door. "Shh. Someone might hear you. And I had to. If we hadn't fought for real, they would have known. You're the one who told me that."

Quentin took the ice pack back and raised it to his black eye. "No one's home. And I know I told you that. I just didn't expect you to hit me so hard. Or so many times." He went to his dresser and grabbed some clothes. "I'm going to shower."

It was probably a good idea. Quentin had a bloody lip, and his clothes were dirty.

"I'm sorry," Hunter said, but Quentin had already left the room.

While Quentin showered in the bathroom by their rooms, Hunter went to grab clean clothes and shower in the master bath. He'd used Ranulf and Chase's bathroom before when the other bathroom was being used.

When he left, he dropped his dirty clothes off in his bedroom and went to Quentin's to check on him. The door was closed, so he knocked.

"Come in."

The scent of soap and wolf-shifter filled the air. "I wanted to check on you before going to bed."

"I'll be fine." Quentin rolled onto his back and winced, but he tried to hide it.

"What's wrong?"

"It's nothing."

Hunter stepped farther into the room. "It's not nothing. Tell me."

"No."

"If you don't spit it out, I'm going to kick your ass again."

Quentin curled his lip at Hunter. "You didn't kick my ass. It was almost a tie."

Hunter moved closer. "I still won," he pointed out.

Quentin seemed to have given up because he rolled away from Hunter and said, "Lift up my shirt. I couldn't see very well in the mirror, so I should probably have someone look at it anyway."

Hunter sat down on the bed and slowly lifted Quentin's shirt. On Quentin's beautiful, dark skin was a giant bruise on the side and back of his ribs. Hunter had to bite his lip, so he didn't make any noises. "Oh, Quentin," still managed to escape past his lips.

"It's pretty bad, isn't it?"

"Did I do this?"

Quentin shook his head. "No. It was when that Tank guy tackled me to the ground."

"Let me get you another ice pack."

Hunter hurried down to the basement where the deep

freezer was kept and found a couple more ice packs. On his way back upstairs, he stopped in the kitchen and grabbed some ibuprofen to help with the swelling.

By the time he got back upstairs, he saw that Quentin had dozed off. Hunter gently shook him awake.

"Huh?"

"I brought you some medicine." Hunter put the pills in Quentin's hand and offered him the water bottle he'd also brought up.

Satisfied Quentin had swallowed the meds, Hunter sat down beside him and put the ice pack on Quentin's side.

Quentin hissed.

"I'm sorry. Am I hurting you?"

"No. Just cold. I wasn't ready for it."

"Are you okay now?"

"Yeah."

Hunter took his hand away from Quentin. "I should probably go."

"Please stay."

"Are you sure? What about Jeremiah?"

Quentin chuckled. "I'm not sure he'll be in the picture much longer."

"You told him, huh?"

"Yeah. He needs to think things over."

"I'm sorry."

Quentin lifted a shoulder. "It is what it is."

Hunter lay down next to Quentin and put his hand back on the ice pack. "I can hold that for you."

Quentin scooted backward until Hunter was spooning him. "Thanks. If you want, the remote to my TV is behind you. I know you're probably not going to sleep like I am."

"Thanks, but I'm okay."

"Just don't leave."

Hunter had no idea why Quentin wanted him to stay so

badly, but he wasn't going to go anywhere. "I'll be here when you wake up."

When Quentin didn't answer, Hunter lifted his head to see Quentin had already fallen asleep.

Hunter laid his head back down and wrapped his arm around the wolf-shifter. If he was going to stay with Quentin the rest of the night, he might as well get comfortable.

☾

"Are you sure this is where Monica is?" Raven asked Chase.

He checked his phone. "This is the address that Lachlan sent me. He said her phone is pinging here. And this *is* her address. Maybe she's sleeping."

It might be the address he had been given, but there was nothing going on in that house tonight. The lights were out, and the air around it was silent.

"Maybe text him again," Ranulf suggested.

"Okay, but he's with Damien tonight. He might not answer right away," Chase said.

Ranulf looked at Raven in the backseat. "Maybe you should text Monica again. Ask her what she's doing tonight."

"I can't do that now. It's the middle of the night. I should have asked her hours ago." But earlier, they had assumed they'd be able to find Monica and follow her if she went somewhere.

Ranulf shrugged, not bothered that she'd put down his idea.

"You could always pretend like you're drunk."

Raven thought about this. "I don't know. It seems weird that I would drunk-text someone I don't know that well."

Chase looked up from his phone. "Not if she's at the top of your list of people you've messaged recently."

Chase did have a point, and she even opened Monica's

message thread, but she hesitated. She had a feeling it was a bad idea.

"You're overthinking," Ranulf said.

Chase reached into the backseat and grabbed her phone. "I'll do it."

"I don't think it's a good idea," Raven told him.

"It's fine."

Chase typed something out, and Raven sighed. She hoped she wasn't going to regret letting him do this.

Chase handed the phone back, and she read what he had written, "*Giiiiirllll, what are you doin?* Five *i*'s and four *l*'s in *girl*. No letter *g* in *doing*."

Chase held out his arms in emphasis. "Yeah. You're drunk, remember?"

Raven continued, "*I'm leavin the bar. Wanted to see if could hang. Call me.*" She slammed her phone down. "Call me, Chase? Now, if she calls, I'll have to act like I'm drunk."

"You'll be fine. She's not going to call."

"I hope you're right."

Five seconds later, Raven's phone beeped, and Chase smiled triumphantly.

"You don't even know if it's her," Raven pointed out.

Chase shrugged. "Why don't you look then?"

Raven glanced down. "Jerk."

Chase and Ranulf laughed.

"What did she say?" Ranulf asked.

"She's busy tonight, but maybe next weekend will work."

"She's busy, but there are no lights on in her house," Chase said, deep in thought. He looked at Ranulf. "You know what that means?" Chase said as he opened the passenger door.

Ranulf was getting out of the driver's side.

"No," Raven said, "what does it mean?"

"That we can take a look around. If she's busy and awake, then why is her house completely dark with no movement? It looks and sounds like she's not home even though her phone says she is." Chase shut his door.

Raven scrambled out of the vehicle. "Uh...she's going to smell us if we go in her house."

"We're not going in," Ranulf said, going to the back of the SUV and opening it. He pulled out three flashlights and a scent eliminator used for deer hunting. "We're going to stay outside and look through the windows. By the time she comes home, our scents should be long gone."

"I sure hope you're right." Raven grabbed a flashlight and let Ranulf spray her clothes.

TWENTY-TWO

QUENTIN OPENED his eyes and groaned as he rolled onto his back. He'd had a number done on him last night. He still couldn't believe Hunter had beaten him in a fight. He hadn't realized until last night that he'd always seen himself as the stronger of the two of them.

Speaking of Hunter, he was fast asleep on Quentin's bed with a book open on his chest. The lamp next to the bed was still on, and he could see some puffiness on Hunter's lip. It made Quentin feel good to know he hadn't taken his ass-kicking without a fight, but it made him sad to see Hunter hurt. It was especially hard, knowing he was the one who'd caused it.

Hunter took a deep breath. "What time is it?" he asked without opening his eyes.

Quentin checked his alarm clock. "It's a little after four."

"And why are you staring at me?"

Quentin smiled. "Checking you over for injuries."

"I'm fine. Better off than you."

Quentin snorted. "Don't remind me."

Hunter's lids slowly lifted, and he stared at Quentin with his blue-green eyes. "Are you okay?"

"Yes. I'll live. I'm a fast healer, as you know. And, hey, at least I didn't get hit by a car."

Hunter smiled at Quentin's joke.

Over a year ago, before Quentin had moved to Switzerland, Hunter had been deliberately hit by a car. He'd been knocked unconscious and left out in the sun with a broken leg.

Quentin met Hunter's eyes. "I probably shouldn't tell you this, but that was one of the worst days of my life."

"Wh—" Hunter cleared his throat. "Why?"

"Because I hated—*hate*—seeing you hurt. I don't like to admit it, but I'm glad Bram is dead; otherwise, I might just have killed him myself."

Hunter slid his book off his chest and rolled onto his side to face Quentin. "I really want to kiss you right now."

"So, kiss me."

"What about Jeremiah? What about us being only friends?"

"We can still be friends."

Hunter raised his eyebrow. "And Jeremiah?"

"Jeremiah and I are on a break right now."

"Does Jeremiah know this? Is he going to end up being the Rachel in this situation?"

Quentin laughed. "Shut up," he said and pulled Hunter down to his mouth.

He cupped Hunter's cheek as he opened his mouth and sucked on Hunter's tongue. He tasted like no one Quentin had ever kissed before. He tasted better than anyone.

Quentin's dick grew hard, and he groaned as he deepened the kiss. Hunter ran his hands over Quentin's hair and rested his weight on him.

Quentin grunted in pain, and Hunter snapped into a sitting position.

"What's wrong? Did I hurt you?" Hunter asked, panicked.

Stupid, sore body.

"Technically, yes, but I don't care about that. Kiss me again."

Hunter's eyes saddened. "I wish I could heal your bruises like I can with open wounds."

Quentin grinned.

Hunter gave him the side-eye. "Why are you smiling like that?"

"Help me take off my shirt." Quentin tried not to wince visibly as Hunter helped him pull off his shirt. He dropped back down to the bed with a sigh but managed to catch Hunter staring at his chest.

Quentin bit his lip and ran his hand down from his neck to his shorts.

Hunter watched, licking his lips.

Quentin's dick jumped under his clothes.

Hunter slowly raised his gaze to Quentin's. "I think you're trying to kill me."

"Not even close. But I am in need of your healing."

Hunter smiled. "Okay."

"It's going to be a lot of work."

"Bring it on."

Quentin pointed to the corner of his mouth. "I split my lip." He ran his finger down the side of his neck. "I have a scratch here." He patted the side opposite of his bruise. "I have a cut on my side. I think Tank had a rock stuck in his shoe when he stepped on me." Quentin pushed the seam of his shorts down, right up to the top of his dick. He tapped his pelvis. "And I somehow got nicked right here."

Hunter raised his eyebrows. "Is that it?"

Quentin pretended to think about it. "Yep. That covers it."

Hunter interlocked his fingers and pushed his hands inside out, cracking his knuckles. He then cracked his neck, stretching it out to the right and then to the left. "Okay. I think I'm ready."

Quentin had purposely laid out his wounds from his neck down, thinking Hunter would take the same path, but he surprised him when he licked Quentin's lower abdomen first.

Quentin had definitely not been ready, so he couldn't help when his shaft jumped again, hitting Hunter on the side of the face.

He groaned, this time for a different kind of pain. "Don't mind him. He's an attention whore."

Hunter lifted his head and crawled up Quentin's body. "I won't." He put his mouth on Quentin's side and sucked and ran his tongue over his wound there.

"Oh God," Quentin muttered.

Hunter moved further up to Quentin's neck and nipped at his vein before taking care of his wound.

"Bite me."

"No," Hunter said next to his ear. "You don't need to be losing blood right now."

"I'm fin—"

Hunter kissed him again but made sure to pay special attention to the cut on his lip.

When Quentin was pretty much a puddle of horniness, Hunter lifted his head.

"Okay, I'm done. How are you feeling?" Hunter sounded so nonchalant that if it wasn't for the giant erection in the front of his pants, Quentin would have thought the vampire was immune to him.

"Better."

Hunter smiled. "Good." He snapped his fingers. "You know what?"

"What?"

"I think I forgot one spot." Hunter slid back down Quentin's body, pulled down his shorts, and sucked his dick into his mouth.

TWENTY-THREE

HUNTER RELUCTANTLY RELEASED Quentin's cock from his mouth but gave the head one last kiss before he let go. He pulled Quentin's shorts back up, so the wolf was covered again.

He collapsed on the bed and used his feet to push himself up, so his head would be next to Quentin's.

Quentin was lying still with his eyes closed.

"Are you okay?"

For a second, he wondered if he'd done a bad job, but Quentin had been making some encouraging noises while Hunter gave him head.

"Yeah," Quentin answered. "Just waiting for my soul to come back into my body."

Hunter laughed, feeling relieved.

Quentin opened his eyes and turned his head. "I think you've gotten better at that."

Hunter put an arm behind his head and stared up at the ceiling. "I'd like to think so."

"Does this mean you've given blow jobs to more than just me?"

"There have been a few here and there."

"Have you—" Quentin cleared his throat. "Have you... done...anything else with anyone?"

"I've had my dick sucked, too."

"I kind of assumed that. I meant, have you…"

It was time to put Quentin out of his misery.

Hunter turned his head and looked at the wolf. "Have I let anyone else fuck me? No."

"And have you…fucked anyone?"

"Not yet." He looked at the ceiling again. "Does that make me some kind of virgin?"

Quentin made a noise that sounded like he was laughing and choking at the same time. "No, you're not a virgin."

"Oh."

"You sound disappointed."

"Nah. I mean, I can't put it on my Tinder profile now, but whatever."

Quentin laughed, and Hunter heard him moving, so he looked over.

"What are you doing?"

"Rolling onto my side."

Hunter sat up on his elbows. "But why? You should lie back down. Your side has to be killing you."

"It hurts. I'm a little sore from lying here for a while, but there is something I need to do."

"What is so important that I can't do it for you?" That was why Hunter was here—to help him.

Quentin got up onto his knees and sat back on his heels. "If you can suck your own dick, I'll give you fifty bucks."

"Okay, you have a point. I can't do that. Can you?"

Quentin frowned. "No."

"Not even when you're a wolf?"

Quentin chuckled. "Yes, I can lick my own balls when I'm in my wolf form. No, I don't give myself BJs." He pushed

Hunter's shoulders until he fell back. "Now, let me take care of you."

Hunter should tell Quentin no. The wolf needed to rest. But he hadn't felt Quentin's mouth on him for way too long. He only had so much strength.

He closed his eyes as Quentin pulled his pants off and down. Quentin ran his hands up Hunter's legs and lay down between his thighs.

Quentin pushed his face into Hunter's pelvis and inhaled. "You smell so good."

Hunter opened his eyes just in time to see Quentin pull his dick into his mouth. His cock twitched the second it hit Quentin's tongue.

Quentin smiled and maneuvered his body, so he could take Hunter all the way to the back of his throat.

"Fuck," Hunter said on an exhale.

Quentin released him. "Who gives the best head?"

Why Quentin cared about this, he didn't know. It was almost as if the wolf was jealous, but maybe he was just competitive.

Quentin licked Hunter's cock from root to tip. "Answer me, Hunter."

"You do," he admitted.

Even if Quentin didn't give the best blow jobs, he would still feel the best to Hunter. No matter what happened, Quentin would always be special to Hunter.

All too soon, Hunter was fisting Quentin's bedding, trying to hold off his climax so the experience wouldn't have to end.

But nothing good lasted forever.

"I'm going to—"

Hunter didn't get to finish as he exploded in Quentin's mouth. He forced his eyes open, so he could watch Quentin's Adam's apple move as he swallowed him.

After his orgasm subsided, Hunter's head fell back against the pillow. "How did I ever think I was asexual?"

Quentin laughed as he came to lie beside him, wincing slightly. "Some people are, so it's not impossible."

"I know. It's just that if I had really thought about it, I would have known that I was attracted to males."

Quentin shrugged. "You probably didn't let yourself even consider it. The mind is a powerful thing."

"That it is."

Quentin put his hand on Hunter's chest. "The important thing is, you know now. You have the rest of your life to live, lusting after men."

Too bad Hunter only lusted after one man. If he could stay there with Quentin forever, just the two of them, life would be perfect.

The sound of the door in the kitchen being opened snapped Hunter back into reality. He flew up. "Shit. Where are my pants?" He scrambled off the bed, but even in his haste to find his clothes, he managed to catch the look of disappointment on Quentin's face.

TWENTY-FOUR

RAVEN STRETCHED out her neck and back while standing in the kitchen. "I think I was crouching in the wrong position for too long. Now, I hurt."

The three of them—Raven, Chase, and Ranulf—hadn't found any huge red flags while searching Monica's property, but a few things had stood out as odd. Monica's home was a modest house in a modest neighborhood. But it was probably a little more than she could spend, based on her salary. Not to mention, the pool and hot tub in her backyard, the big screen TVs she had all around her house, and the designer dresses she had lying on her bed.

And these were only the things they could see from the windows, minus the pool and hot tub. Raven had a feeling if they had gone inside, they would have found a lot more items that showed Monica spent money outside her means.

"Go get ready for bed, and I'll give you a back rub," Chase said.

Raven spun around to see if he had some hidden agenda for offering to help her out, but he was opening the fridge.

"I'm fine," she told him.

Ranulf looked in the pantry. "Are you hungry, Raven?"

"No, thanks."

Chase turned from the fridge. "It's not a big deal. I like giving back rubs."

Ranulf pulled a box out of the pantry and opened it before sniffing the inside and shaking it. "He does. And he's good at it. I wouldn't pass up a massage from him."

If Ranulf got back rubs from Chase, she was probably safe. And she would sleep so much better after she got one. "Okay. I'll see you upstairs then."

"Just come to our room when you're ready. We'll be up when we're done eating."

Raven went upstairs and saw Hunter's door shut just as she got to the top. She thought about telling him hi, but he'd have heard them and known they'd come home. If he had wanted to talk, he would have left his door open.

Quentin's door was also closed, and she knew he had to work in the morning, so she didn't bother going in and filling him in on her night.

She went to her bedroom and changed into something more comfortable to sleep in. She brushed her teeth, washed her face, and headed down to Ranulf and Chase's room. The door was wide open, and neither of them had come upstairs yet, so she grabbed the remote off the table and got on Chase's bed to wait.

A few minutes later, the two of them came upstairs, laughing at something.

"Did I miss a good joke?" she asked as they walked into the room.

"Nah," Ranulf said, pulling off his shirt. "Chase dropped the leftovers Payton's mom left us."

Raven gasped and dragged her eyes away from Ranulf's nice chest. "How could you?"

Payton's mom was the best cook in the state of Minnesota,

and the wolf-shifters loved when she made them food. The cat-shifters didn't know how lucky they were to have her around all the time.

"I caught it," Chase defended himself as he took off his shirt, too. "I only spilled a tiny bit. All is not lost."

"The look on his face was hilarious," Ranulf said, pushing his jeans down.

"Well, yeah. Damien would have been pissed if I had dropped all his mother-in-law's food on the floor," Chase said as he kicked off his pants, too.

Raven closed her eyes and rolled to the side. She should not be getting aroused at a time like this. And if they smelled it, she'd never hear the end of it.

"You okay, Raven?" Chase asked. He sounded genuinely concerned and not at all like he was making fun of her.

"Yeah, I'm fine," she said into his pillow. *Damn, it smells good.* She needed to get out of there.

Raven moved swiftly off the bed but not too fast as to make the guys think she was crazy for leaving so quickly.

They both frowned at her.

"Where are you going?" Ranulf asked.

"Yeah, I thought you wanted a massage."

She almost groaned and stomped her foot because, damn it, she did want that.

"I should go to bed."

She moved past the both of them, but Chase caught her arm and twirled her around. "What's wrong?"

She opened her eyes wide to try and look innocent. "Nothing. I'm just tired."

Ranulf tilted his head and narrowed his eyes. "She's lying."

Raven gasped.

"Oh, I know she is," Chase said.

Ranulf moved nearer to her, leaned over, and inhaled a deep breath.

Raven took a step back, knowing what he'd smell, but ran into Chase, who was now behind her. Ranulf shifted closer, so now, she was between the two males.

Two almost completely naked, only-wearing-boxer-brief males.

She was starting to grow wet between her legs. *Distract.* "What are you—"

"She's horny."

Raven gasped again as Chase swept her hair off to one side and sniffed her neck. "Yeah, she is."

Ranulf brushed a lock of hair off her face. "How long's it been?"

She could play dumb, but she didn't bother. "I haven't been with a man in almost a year."

Ranulf cringed, and Chase made a noise behind her.

She stepped out from between the two of them. "You guys make it seem like it's horrible. We don't all have to have sex that often."

"Yeah, we do," they both said at the same time.

Raven rolled her eyes and crossed her arms over her chest. "Okay, so I know I need some physical contact, but sex isn't everything."

Chase came over to her and nudged her toward his bed. "That's one more reason why you need a back rub. You can get some physical contact to make your wolf happy without sex."

He did have a good point.

"Okay." She whipped her finger up and pointed at him. "But no funny business."

Chase smiled. "Only if you ask me real nice."

"Ha-ha. I won't." At least, she didn't think she would.

"Take off your shirt and get on the bed." Chase turned around, and Ranulf followed. "We won't look."

Raven yanked off her shirt and lay facedown on Chase's bed. "Ready."

"Okay. I need to grab a few things, and then I'll start," Chase said.

Raven heard a drawer open and a few things being moved around before the bed dipped next to her.

"This might be cold at first, but it will warm up in a few minutes," Chase said.

He poured something onto her back, smeared it around, and then began massaging.

Ranulf was right. Chase was good at giving massages.

TWENTY-FIVE

RAVEN WOKE SOMETIME LATER, unsure of where she was. She blinked a few times until she realized she was in Chase's bed. She must have fallen asleep during the back rub.

Her shirt was still off, but someone had pulled the covers up over her.

And she was alone.

She quietly sat up, keeping the sheet in front of her chest, and looked around. She could see someone in Ranulf's bed but couldn't tell if it was him or Chase from where she was.

But whoever it was seemed to be sleeping, so she dropped the bedding and stood up to look. She felt bad for kicking Chase out of his bed. She hadn't meant to. And she wouldn't have cared if he'd slept next to her.

Despite her acting like she wanted to get away from both of the males earlier, it was only because she had been horny and hadn't wanted to let herself get caught up in their sexiness.

Normally, she wouldn't care if she slept in the same bed as any of the male wolf-shifters in the house. They were like one big, weird family, and they were shifters. They were pack animals.

But she was scared to get involved with Ranulf and Chase on a sexual level. There were two of them and only one of her. In the end, she would be the one hurt when things ended while they would still have each other.

As she got to the edge of the bed, she saw that both Chase and Ranulf were sleeping in Ranulf's bed. Those two were definitely non-sexual life partners. At least, non-sexual with each other.

She giggled for some reason, and Chase stirred.

"Hey, Raven."

She jumped and made a squeak sound. "Oh shit, you scared me."

"Sorry." He tugged on her wrist. "Come and sleep with us."

For some reason, she forgot all her reservations about staying away from the two of them because she lifted a shoulder and said, "Okay."

She knew she'd be hot, sleeping in the middle of two big males, so she pushed her pants off and climbed over Chase to get into bed.

Chase pulled the covers over her, and she settled in with her back to his chest and her chest to Ranulf's back. It was cozy and warm, and even though she could take care of herself, she felt safe. It was the perfect combination.

She closed her eyes and tried to go back to sleep, but she soon became aware that both of them smelled incredibly good. And that they were almost as naked as she was. She actually pictured the three of them messing around.

It was then that she knew she was going to need a bit more than physical contact for her wolf to be satisfied, and she actually considered waiting until Chase fell back to sleep before touching herself.

No. Bad Raven. You cannot masturbate next to Ranulf and Chase.

She wanted to cry because she was going to have to get up

and leave. There was no way she was falling asleep in between the two.

Ranulf rolled over and looked her in the eye. She had thought he was asleep.

"Baby girl, why don't you just let us take care of you?"

Baby girl was what Damien called Payton, and Raven couldn't help getting a little *aw* feeling inside her chest upon hearing Ranulf call her that.

"I…"

"*I* what?"

"I don't know."

Ranulf ran his hand up her side and flicked her nipple.

She moaned.

"Do you want more of that? Because you smell like you do," Ranulf said.

Chase's hand came up from behind her and cupped her breast. "You smell like sex on steroids."

"I'm sorry," Raven said.

Ranulf shook his head in disappointment. "Don't ever be sorry. Your sex is the best fucking thing I've smelled in forever." And with that, he pulled the covers over his head and moved down toward the foot of the bed.

"What's he doing?"

Chase kissed her neck and pulled on her nipple. "You'll see."

Ranulf ran his hand up her leg until he got to her underwear. She felt his hand shift into a paw, and her underwear fell to each side. He must have used a claw to cut them. He cut another spot, and almost like magic, her underwear was gone.

Chase continued to suck and kiss her neck and shoulder as Ranulf lifted her leg and pushed his mouth between her thighs. He wasn't hesitant or meek about it. He dived right in, which was such a turn-on for Raven.

And it was a good thing he'd shifted his paw back into his

hand because he grabbed her ass and actually tried to bring her pussy closer to his mouth. He ate her out like he was trying to win a contest.

And it felt amazing. His cheeks were rough against her thighs, but his lips and tongue were soft. Ranulf could be a tour guide on how to get to the clitoris. He narrowed in on that spot between her legs and massaged it with his tongue.

Meanwhile, Chase was working her neck and her nipples. She was one big orgasm ready to combust. It was when Chase bit down on her neck that she could no longer hold back, and she exploded.

Ranulf kissed his way up her stomach and pulled her nipple into his mouth. Raven whimpered, and Ranulf threw the covers off his head.

"Holy shit, Chase, she tastes even better than she smells."

Chase moved from behind her, and Ranulf pushed her onto her back as Chase pulled the covers down.

They each moved one of her legs apart, and her arousal filled the room even more.

"Damn, you are sexy," Ranulf said and pushed two fingers inside her.

She whimpered again.

"Soft and responsive." He pulled his hand away and stuck his fingers in his mouth to suck off her flavor. "Your turn," he said to Chase.

Chase moved between her legs and got down on his belly.

"You don't have—" *To do that*, she was going to say before Ranulf silenced her with a kiss.

They'd already given her an orgasm. They didn't have to give her another.

But Chase was already going down on her. He slid a finger or two inside her and went right for her G-spot. If Ranulf was going to be the tour guide, Chase was going to be his right-hand man.

Ranulf broke their kiss to focus on her breasts. He used his mouth on her nipples like he had her clit, and soon, she was ready to come again. She had her hand in Ranulf's hair, and she was pretty sure she was hurting him, but he didn't complain.

Chase lifted his head for a moment to say, "She likes it when you bite her neck."

Ranulf kissed his way up her neck and whispered next to her ear, "Is that true?"

"I don't know," she whined.

"Only one way to find out." Ranulf tilted her head and kissed her neck, and then he licked before he sucked until, finally, he bit down.

And Chase was right. She went off again like a rocket.

By the time both of the males lay down again beside her, she was a puddle of nothing, and she had no strength to even lift a pinkie finger.

Ranulf grabbed the covers for the bed and pulled it over the three of them.

"What about you two?" Raven asked as her eyes started closing. "It's not fair."

Ranulf gave her a kiss on the cheek. "This wasn't about us."

Chase kissed her on the other cheek. "This was about you."

"You guys are sweet," she muttered.

"Sweet? She just called us sweet, man," Chase said.

Ranulf chuckled. "It's a compliment."

"Okay, I'll let it go. But if she calls us sweet after we fuck her, I'm changing my mind."

"I'm not fucking you," Raven said into the pillow.

"Sure you are, babe," Chase said.

"You just don't know it yet," Ranulf finished.

Whatever you say, is what she tried to tell them, but it didn't make it past her thoughts. Instead, she fell into a blissful, dreamless sleep.

TWENTY-SIX

"*QUENTIN,*" one of his commanding officers barked at him.

"Sir?" He usually wasn't so lost in his thoughts, but he couldn't forget the look of panic in Hunter's eyes when he'd realized someone else was in the house last night.

"A detective wants to talk to you."

"Hmm?"

The officer clapped his hands. "Focus, Rawling. A detective wants to speak with you."

Quentin frowned. "Me? Why?"

"Why don't you go and find out? He's waiting for you in interrogation room two."

Shaking all thoughts of Hunter from his mind, he went in search of the detective who was seeking out an officer. The actual room where they questioned criminals was empty, but the room next to it where the police could watch through the one-way mirror was occupied by a dark-haired man. He was scrolling through his phone and writing on a notepad.

Quentin rapped his knuckles on the open door.

The dark-haired man looked up. "Officer Quentin Rawling?"

Quentin stepped inside and held out his hand. "That's me."

The man shook his hand, and Quentin smelled cat-shifter. But there was also a familiarity that he couldn't quite figure out.

"Detective Eldon Conrad. Do you mind shutting the door behind you?"

Quentin did as he had been asked because even if he had never met the guy, the detective outranked him.

"Have we met before?"

"No. Why do you ask?"

Maybe he was mistaken about his scent. "No reason." He looked around the room. "Can I ask what this is about?"

"Where were you last night?"

The detective should have no idea where he had been last night, but Quentin had a feeling the cat-shifter already knew. This was not good.

Quentin cleared his throat. "With all due respect, sir, I'd rather not say."

"And why would that be?"

"I plead the fifth."

Detective Conrad tapped his pen on his chin. "What if I promised that you wouldn't be in trouble and that I only wanted your help?"

Quentin took this into consideration. Since the detective seemed to already know where he'd been and hadn't thrown the book at him, there was a chance he was telling the truth. He spread his legs and squared his shoulders, ready to take whatever punishment was coming his way.

"I was at a fight club, sir."

"Did you participate?"

"Not willingly, sir."

"And why were you there?"

"To help a friend."

"And are you planning on going back?"

"No, sir." As long as he could keep Hunter away.

"What if I told you I wanted you to go back?"

Quentin's shoulders fell as his resolve turned to confusion. "Sir?"

There was a table in the room, and Detective Conrad sat on the edge. "Look, shifter to shifter, I've been trying to track down this fighting ring for some time. I finally got an undercover officer in but only as a bystander. He hasn't even had a chance to make any bets yet. But the UC called and told me that he recognized you last night."

Quentin blew out a deep breath and rocked on his heels. He had been so caught up in Hunter that he'd never even thought to see if he recognized anyone in the crowd.

"So, tell me, Officer Rawling, were you really there, helping a friend, or are you in some deep shit? Because I could really use some good news today."

"I really was there, helping a friend. I got caught, sneaking around, and they forced me to fight."

Conrad laughed. "Yeah, I heard how you got tackled."

"And I'm sure you heard how I lost the fight, too." Quentin didn't like to think he had a big ego, but he didn't like everyone knowing he'd lost.

"Yeah, I did. But I think that can work to our advantage. See, you losing will give you a good reason to go back and fight again."

"It's not my place, but why don't you just arrest these guys?"

"Because we don't have all the details yet and we're not sure if they're actually the ones in charge. We think the operation is bigger than just the fighting ring. We believe that the two guys who run the fights are part of a smaller organization that is actually behind more serious crimes. We think they answer to someone, and these fights are just the tip of the iceberg. And that's why we need a contact on the inside to gain their trust." He stood. "So, tell me about this friend. Is he going to be a problem? Is he trustworthy? Can we bring him in as an informant?"

Quentin laughed.

"Sorry, I missed the joke."

"He's a Guardian, so I think he's probably the best informant you can get."

"A Guardian. As in a vampire Guardian?"

Quentin nodded.

Conrad whistled. "I wasn't expecting that." His brow furrowed. "What the hell was he doing there in the first place?"

Quentin opened his mouth to answer, but then he realized he didn't actually know. That was something he'd neglected to ask Hunter about last night. "This is going to sound like the lamest answer, sir, but I don't know. In the midst of everything, I forgot to ask him. But if I'm being honest, I know he's gone there more than once."

Conrad raised his brow. "He does know they're illegal, right?"

"Yeah, he knows."

"And I can't imagine the vampires are okay with something like this."

"I'm sure they're not."

"Well, if he cooperates, I can keep his little secret."

Quentin smiled even though the situation wasn't really funny.

"What joke am I missing now?" Conrad asked.

"There is no way you're going to be able to keep it a secret."

"And why is that?"

"If you want me and Hunter—my friend—to help you, we need to get permission from Damien Lowell."

"Damien Lowell? The wolf-shifter alpha?"

"The one and only."

"And why do we need his permission?"

"Because Hunter is living with the wolf-shifters and I am one of the wolf-shifter sentinels."

"Oh shit."

"Yeah."

"Is this going to be a problem?"

Quentin thought about how Damien was going to react. "I don't think so, but…"

"He has no clue where you were last night, does he?"

"Nope."

"I guess we'll see what he thinks tonight."

"Tonight?" Quentin asked.

"Yeah. After work, you and I can go talk to him together. What time is your shift over?"

"Seven."

"I'll be back here by then."

TWENTY-SEVEN

RAVEN WOKE up to someone kicking the bed again.

She opened one eye to see Kendall staring down at her, just like the other morning.

"What?" Raven asked.

Kendall raised her eyebrows. "Really? You have to ask?"

Raven closed her eye. "Yes. I'm tired."

"You're naked in Ranulf's bed."

Raven flew up so fast that she forgot to grab the sheet that had been covering her breasts.

"Damn, girl. You look like you had a rough night."

Raven lifted the covers to her chest and looked around the room. It was only her and Kendall. "Where are they?"

She didn't have to tell Kendall who "they" were. She knew Raven meant Chase and Ranulf.

"They left to run an errand about fifteen minutes ago."

Raven dropped the sheet and climbed out of bed. Her shirt was on the floor next to Chase's bed, where she had dropped it after taking it off before he gave her a massage. Thankfully, it went to mid-thigh because she had no idea where her underwear was.

Kendall lifted a scrap of fabric off the floor and held it up. "Are you looking for these?" She twisted them around. "I don't think they'll be of much use to you, seeing as how they're broken."

Raven took a giant step toward her friend and tried to snatch them out of her grip. "I'll take those."

Kendall was too fast. She whipped her hand behind her back. With her free hand, she wagged her finger at Raven. "Uh-uh-uh. Not until you tell me what happened last night." She grinned. "Did you have sex with them?" She closed her eyes, looking pained. "Please tell me you had sex with them." She lifted her lids. "I haven't had sex since I got pregnant. I think I'm reaching some sort of weird pregnancy sexual heat because I want to hear everything. I'm so horny."

"And if nothing happened?"

"I'd call you a lying liar because your nipples are red, you have bite marks on both sides of your neck, and it smells like pussy in here, Raven. Pussy."

Raven pulled the hem of her shirt down. She wasn't normally self-conscious, but Kendall had noticed way too much. "I don't know if I should tell you, you big weirdo."

"Please. I need to live vicariously through you. Did you not hear how horny I am?"

"If you promise to stop saying *horny*, I'll tell you."

"Horny, horny, horny." She grabbed Raven's hand and smacked the ripped underwear into her palm. "Okay, I'm done. Now, tell me."

Raven nodded toward the door. "Let's go to my room."

Kendall looked around as if she'd just remembered where they were. "Good point."

"How were the cat-shifters?" Raven asked as they walked to her room.

"Good. They said to tell everyone hi."

After living with the cat-shifters for months, Kendall had

become friends with most of them, and sometimes, she hung out with them for the night. Since no one from the wolf-shifters had replaced her there, she still had a room and would often spend the night.

"I'm glad you got out of the house a little."

They reached Raven's room, and Kendall shut the door behind them. "Okay. No more talk about my lonely adventures last night. I want to hear about you."

Raven smiled and felt a little dirty for playing kiss and tell, but she also knew she could trust Kendall with a secret. "I didn't have sex."

Kendall's smile fell. "That sucks."

Raven laughed. "But they did both go down on me." She grinned knowingly. "And they both made me come."

Kendall walked over to Raven's bed and fell onto it with her hand on her chest. "That sounds amazing."

Raven smiled as she went to find some clean clothes to wear. "It was. Don't tell them though."

Kendall sat up as fast as her belly would let her. "Oh, I would *never*. Those two don't need anything added to their egos."

"Thanks."

"So, how did it happen?"

Raven told Kendall about the stakeout and searching Monica's house. And that Chase had offered to give her a back rub when they got home and how she'd fallen asleep in his bed. "They both knew my wolf needed some physical contact, and one thing led to another."

Kendall sighed dreamily as if Raven had just told her how they'd proposed to her. Kendall really must be horny.

"Do you think they'd help a pregnant woman out? I could really use a couple of non-self-induced orgasms right about now."

Raven turned her head back to her closet before Kendall

could see her face. The image of Chase and Ranulf being intimate with Kendall made Raven want to punch something.

"What's wrong?" Kendall asked.

Raven looked at her friend. "Huh?"

"You were growling."

Shit. That wasn't good.

"Oh, I just realized I forgot to wash some clothes. And I really don't feel like doing it."

Kendall looked like she didn't believe Raven. "Okay. You know, I'm happy to help. I don't do much around here anyway."

Raven really didn't expect Kendall to do her laundry, but she was still a little irked at Kendall's comment, so she pulled her basket out of her closet. "If you really want to do it, here are my dirty clothes."

Kendall laughed.

"What's so funny?"

Kendall shook her head. "Nothing." She got up from Raven's bed and walked over to her. She put her arm around Raven and gave her a side hug. "Don't worry. I won't do anything with Ranulf and Chase."

"Okay. But I don't care."

Kendall lifted her head and walked toward the door. "Whatever you say, Raven."

"It's true," Raven shouted as Kendall walked out. "I really don't care."

There was no response from Kendall.

TWENTY-EIGHT

ELDON CONRAD FOLLOWED Quentin Rawling into the big house that he lived in with a handful of other wolf-shifters.

"Does your vampire friend live with you and one of your sentinels lives with them?"

Quentin did a double take. "How did you know that?"

"Oh, I worked with the cat-shifters with some help from the wolves some months back. But I don't remember you."

He did remember a certain dark-haired wolf-shifter who had left a lasting impression on him though. He hadn't been able to forget about her all this time. It was a good thing she lived with the cats because he didn't know what he'd do if he saw her again. Something between pretending like he barely remembered her to throwing her over his shoulder and taking her to bed.

Because those two options were so close to the same thing. That was how fucked up he was over her.

"I was out of the country on family business for almost a year."

"That would explain it."

Eldon wondered how many of the wolf-shifters would

remember him. And he wondered how many knew he'd slept with Kendall.

They walked through the door at the back of the house and into the kitchen. Eldon hadn't realized he'd been holding his breath until he saw that it was empty.

"Hey," Quentin called out. "Anyone home?"

A black-haired cat-shifter walked into the kitchen. "Hey, Quentin. Almost everyone is upstairs."

"Damien, too?"

"Yes, but he should be down any second."

"Payton, this is Eldon Conrad."

She held out her hand to Eldon to shake. "Yes, I remember you. We met briefly after you and Kendall escaped."

Quentin's eyes widened, and recognition dawned in them. "Oh shit. You're that cat-shifter. I heard all about you when I was in Europe."

"Yeah, you missed a lot, Quentin," Payton said. "Speaking of missing a lot, I'll be right back."

"Tell Damien to hurry, will you?"

Payton was already out of the room.

"Are you hungry? Can I get you anything to eat?" Quentin asked, walking to the other side of the room and opening the fridge.

"No, I'm good. I picked up something on my way back to your station tonight."

"Good, because I have no idea what kind of food we have around here. There has been talk of hiring someone to cook for us, but so far, that's all it's been."

Eldon smiled, grateful that he had thought to eat before coming there tonight, when a scent caught his nose. Two scents actually. One familiar and one not, but it sure made alarm bells go off in his head.

As if in slow motion, he turned his head just as Kendall walked into the kitchen.

"Quentin, Payton told me to come down here." She sounded confused until she took a single whiff of the air and spun in Eldon's direction.

Her eyes grew to the size of plates when she saw him.

Eldon was frozen in place, staring at her face until her hands moved in front of her belly in a bad attempt to hide it.

He felt all the blood rush out of his head as his vision went black, and he reached out for something to steady himself. All he encountered was air.

☾

"Quentin, help. He's going down." There was no way, in her condition, that Kendall could hold him up by herself.

Quentin spun around and raced from the fridge to Eldon, barely catching him before the cat-shifter's head hit the floor. "Holy shit, what's wrong with him?"

Kendall smiled uncertainly. "He just found out I was pregnant."

Quentin looked confused. "And that matters because?"

She laughed nervously. "Because the baby is his."

"That would do it."

☾

Eldon opened his eyes and began assessing his surroundings. He didn't know what was going on, but his cop instincts told him something wasn't right.

"You're in my room."

He jerked his head around to the doorway where Kendall stood, and everything came back to him.

She was fucking pregnant. And he'd fainted. *How embarrassing.*

He slowly sat up as she came and took a seat beside him.

She tried to smile at him. "I suppose you'd like an explanation."

"That would be nice."

She put her hand on top of her round belly. "First off, as you probably know, it's yours."

He snorted. "Yeah, I figured."

He was going to be a father.

And his vision started to narrow again.

He dropped his head between his legs before he passed out again.

He'd seen dead fucking bodies and horrific crime scenes and not batted an eye, but he found out he was going to have a kid and became a freaking wimp.

"I'm sorry. I didn't mean for you to find out like this."

That was enough for him to gather the strength to lift his head. "Or do you mean, ever?"

She leaned back at his remark, but she kind of deserved it. He hadn't seen her for seven months. That meant she only had two to go before she gave birth. It wasn't like she hadn't had plenty of time to tell him.

She took a deep breath. "Okay, I know you're upset, so I'll let that go."

He laughed. "*Upset* doesn't even begin to cover how I feel. Why the fuck would you keep this from me?"

"I don't know, Eldon. We chose to make a clean break from one another because of what had happened with your brother."

His brother had locked up both him and Kendall because he had gotten involved with a bad group of shifters who considered themselves purists. Because Eldon had convinced his alpha to turn his brother over to the police, he and Kendall had decided it was best to stay away from each other, so the police wouldn't know she had been involved, and they wouldn't risk shifter information getting out.

"And truth be told, I don't know you that well. I didn't know how you'd react, and I didn't want you to feel like you had to do something about it."

"*It* being the baby?"

She lifted a shoulder. "The baby. The pregnancy."

"That wasn't your decision to make, Kendall. You should have told me. The thing with my brother was months ago. The case is closed. He pled guilty, so there was no trial. No one would think to tie you to what happened."

She looked down at her hands. "I already said I was sorry."

"But are you? Really?"

She defiantly lifted her head. "Yes."

He looked at her stomach again. He wanted to touch it. "Where do we go from here?"

"Can I have your hand?"

He lifted his arm, and she took his hand in hers as she scooted closer to him. She put it low on her belly.

"Wait a second," she whispered.

"What am I waiting for?" he asked.

Bam. He felt something hit his hand.

His eyes rounded, and Kendall laughed.

"He kicked. Usually, whenever someone tries to feel, he stops. That's why I whispered."

"Will he do it again?" Eldon asked in a low voice, following her lead.

"Talk in a normal voice again. I think he likes it."

He met her eyes. "What should I say?"

She shrugged. "I don't know. Anything."

"Is it really a boy, or are you just using masculine pronouns?"

Boom. Another kick. And another.

Kendall's face lit up. "I think he likes you." She looked down and back up again, this time a little shy. "And, yes, he's a boy. I plan to call him Conrad."

TWENTY-NINE

QUENTIN WAS STILL STUNNED from the news that a male he'd just met that day was the father of Kendall's baby. It was a lot to process on top of the undercover mission Conrad wanted him to go on and the fact he and Hunter still needed to talk to Damien about what had happened.

He put his dirty dishes in the dishwasher and went in search of Hunter. He should talk to the vampire first, so they could talk to Damien together.

He went upstairs and could hear Eldon and Kendall having a conversation in her room as he walked past. He made sure to block them out so as not to eavesdrop on what was being said even though he could imagine it would be quite the story to tell others later.

Quentin kept walking until he reached Hunter's door and knocked. There was no answer, so he knocked again, louder this time.

There was still no response from the other side, so Quentin slowly opened the door. The lights were out, and Hunter was in bed, which was odd. Hunter was usually up by now even if it was summer and the sun was still out.

Of course, Quentin hadn't lived here in a long time. Maybe Hunter slept in more.

Or maybe Quentin had worn Hunter out last night. He couldn't help but smile at the thought and feel a little proud of himself.

"Hunter."

The vampire didn't stir, so Quentin stepped inside.

He moved closer and repeated his name again, "Hunter."

When he reached Hunter's bed without any movement, Quentin's heart was racing, and his palms were starting to sweat. He shook Hunter's shoulder.

He'd been lying on his side up until then but flopped onto his back when Quentin touched him. But he didn't wake up.

Quentin ran over to the light switch and flipped it on, so he could see better.

Hunter was pale, and his breathing was uneven. Quentin put two fingers to his neck and watched the clock while counting.

Hunter's heart was racing.

Quentin ran to the door and yelled, "Damien."

Damien yanked open the door to his and Payton's room as he pulled on a shirt. "What's wrong?"

Raven poked her head out of her door at that point, too.

"I don't know. He won't wake up. He has a rapid heart rate, and his breathing is shallow. I think we need to take him to the vampire clinic."

"Shit." Damien came toward Hunter's room just as Kendall's door opened. He halted when he saw both her and the cat-shifter. "Eldon Conrad?"

"Hello again."

Damien glanced down at Kendall's pregnant stomach and at Eldon. He lifted an eyebrow.

"Sounds like there's trouble. How can I help?" Eldon asked.

"Hunter's unresponsive," Quentin answered.

"Payton," Damien yelled.

She appeared right behind him. Quentin hadn't even seen her.

"Call your brother. Have Naya call the vampire clinic and tell them we're on the way."

Payton sprinted back toward their bedroom, presumably to get her phone, while Damien walked into Hunter's bedroom.

"Raven," he shouted. "Zane."

She ran to the door along with Eldon. "Zane and Isabelle aren't here. They're at her parents'."

"Shit, that's right. Raven, I need you to help me bring Hunter downstairs. Eldon, you in? I would like to keep him as still as possible, or I'd just throw him over my shoulder."

"I'm in," Eldon said.

Quentin wasn't sure if they needed four shifters to move one vampire even if they did want to move him carefully. "I'm going to help."

"No, I want you to go and bring a vehicle as close to the door as you can." Damien looked Quentin up and down. "I changed my mind. Raven, I want you to get the vehicle, and, Quentin, you can help bring Hunter downstairs."

"On it," Raven said and ran out of the room.

Payton rushed back into the room. "Damien, Naya's on the phone with the clinic, but Vaughn wants to know if we know what happened to him."

Damien shook his head.

"I think I know," Quentin said. He wasn't one hundred percent sure, but it had to be the reason.

Damien's head spun around, and his eyes narrowed. "What do you know?"

"I think he might have gotten injured from fighting."

"Fighting? What the hell?"

Quentin looked at Payton. "Have Naya tell the clinic they

should check him for everything from a head injury to internal bleeding." He met his alpha's eyes. "I'll explain the whole thing later."

THIRTY

QUENTIN PACED the waiting room at the clinic as his fear for Hunter gradually increased. This was the second time he'd been at the vampire clinic while Hunter was in a hospital bed, and it was one of the worst feelings in the world. He was so scared Hunter was going to die.

To keep his mind off Hunter dying, Quentin ran the night before over and over in his head, but he couldn't place when Hunter had gotten injured.

Their fight had seemed fair. Hell, Hunter had won. Quentin wasn't an expert, but he didn't think he'd hit Hunter anywhere that would cause such damage as for him to not wake up.

And once they'd arrived home, Hunter had seemed fine. Quentin was the one who had been hurt. Quentin hadn't noticed that Hunter was even trying to hide something like an injury, and he felt like he was pretty good at noticing when Hunter tried to cover up getting hurt.

The doctor walked into the waiting room, and Quentin made a beeline for her. Her name tag read Dr. Montgomery.

Damien and Dante rose from their seats as well, but he barely noticed.

The doctor pulled off her scrub cap. "Hunter's out of surgery. He had a brain bleed that needed repairing."

Quentin's knees felt weak, and he wasn't sure how long he could stay standing. "Brain bleed? How did we not notice?"

"It was a slow bleed," the doctor explained. "He probably had no idea he was hurt when it started. And then he went to sleep, so he missed any symptoms."

Quentin felt like he was going to throw up.

"But the good news is, we caught it in time, and he'll make a full recovery."

"That's a relief," Dante said.

"Can we see him?" Quentin asked.

"Yes. But keep in mind, he's still unconscious. The meds won't wear off for about fifteen more minutes."

Quentin followed the doctor back to Hunter's room without even asking anyone else if they wanted to go first. He needed to see the vampire with his own eyes to make sure he was okay.

It wasn't until he was in the clinic room that he realized Damien and Dante were behind him, but he quickly forgot about them as he saw Hunter's head wrapped in a white bandage.

Quentin rushed over and took Hunter's hand as he sat down next to him.

Even though the doctor had already said Hunter would make a full recovery, Quentin started chanting, *Please wake up,* in his head.

He'd only remembered punching Hunter in the face once, maybe twice last night, but it seemed it had been enough. And if Hunter died because of him…

He didn't know what he'd do with himself.

Tears filled his eyes, but he quickly brushed them away before anyone else in the room saw them.

"In case I'm not back when he regains consciousness, he should probably feed when he wakes up. Does anyone know the last time he fed?" the doctor asked.

Quentin cleared his throat. "Early Friday morning."

"Oh." The doctor brightened. "That's excellent news. Less than a week ago, so he won't need much, but we should probably still make sure he gets some blood."

"I'll make sure he gets fed," Dante said.

The doctor nodded once. "Good," she said and left the room.

The door closed, and Quentin turned back to Hunter. "I'll feed him."

"I think you've done enough," Dante said.

Obviously, the leader of the Guardians didn't understand this wasn't up for negotiation.

Quentin bared his teeth. "I said, I'll do it."

"No. Hunter—"

Dante didn't get to finish his sentence because Quentin flew off his chair and slammed him up against the wall. Dante was taller and slightly bigger than him, but Quentin didn't care.

"If even a drop of your blood enters his body, I will rip off each of your limbs until Phoenix doesn't recognize you."

Damien quickly stepped between the two of them as best as he could and pushed on Quentin's chest. "Quentin, stand down."

Quentin lowered his head, flared his nostrils, and growled.

"Quentin, I said, stand down."

"Not until he promises not to feed Hunter."

"What the fuck?" Dante said.

"Dante," Damien said, "promise him." He looked over his shoulder at the vampire. "Just do it."

"Fine. I won't feed him," Dante said.

Quentin growled again.

"I promise," Dante added.

Quentin let the vampire go with a shove and went back to Hunter's bedside.

He spared a glance at the two leaders and noted that Damien was speaking in a low voice to Dante. Dante's eyes were wide with shock, but Quentin didn't care what was being said between the two.

He looked back at Hunter and ran his finger down the vampire's cheek. He just wanted Hunter to wake up and say he was okay.

THIRTY-ONE

HUNTER WOKE up with the worst headache of his life. He was groggy as hell, and his eyelids felt like they weighed a hundred pounds.

"Hunter?"

He turned his head toward the voice and squinted. "Quentin?"

"Oh, thank God you recognize me."

"Why wouldn't I recognize you?" He sniffed the air. "Am I in the clinic?" He forced his eyes open all the way and immediately inspected his leg since that was what had gotten him there the last time. His limb looked fine. "Why am I here?"

"You had a brain bleed."

Hunter looked at Quentin. The wolf's eyes were red, and he looked exhausted.

"No shit?"

Quentin laughed. "No shit."

Hunter carefully touched his head, patting it all over. He felt a bandage covering him from the top of his head to above his ears.

"You still have hair. But you might want to shave it to match what they had to take off for your surgery."

"What happened?"

"What's the last thing you remember?"

Hunter grinned as he recalled Quentin giving him a blow job. And now, he was getting hard. He put a hand over his crotch and nodded his head toward it. "I'll give you one guess."

Quentin smiled, but his eyes were still sad. "I can't say I'm disappointed you remember that. What else?"

"Um…someone came home, and I had to quickly find my clothes." He also couldn't forget the look of disappointment on Quentin's face when Hunter had practically sprinted out of his room. "I went to my own room, did a few things, but then I started to get a headache, so I went to bed."

Quentin closed his eyes. "I wish you had told me."

"That I had a headache? It wasn't a big deal."

"This one was. It was probably the first sign that you had a bleed." He dropped his head in his hands. "Why didn't I check on you?" He looked up. "Can you forgive me?"

"For not checking on me?" Hunter was confused. "It's not your job to make sure I'm okay in the middle of the night."

"I still don't know how it happened. I've gone over our fight in my head, around and around, but I can't remember when I hurt you."

Hunter was getting more lost by the second. He held up his hand. "Quentin, you're not making sense. I don't understand half of what you're saying."

Quentin sighed. "You got a brain bleed from fighting. I should have taken care of you like you took care of me. And even though I don't remember hitting you in a way to cause the damage that was done to you, I must have because you're here."

"Ahhh." Now, he understood. He slowly shook his head so as not to make his headache worse. "I don't think it was you."

"What?"

"No offense, but I kicked your ass. I don't think you're the one who did this to me."

Quentin looked stunned. "I will not take offense but only because you just came out of anesthesia. And because you're about to tell me it's not my fault."

"It was the guy I was fighting before you were caught. I sensed something was wrong through your blood, and I turned to look. That's when he hit me and knocked me off my feet."

Quentin slumped back in his chair. "So, it's still my fault." He sat up. "I'm sorry, man. I didn't mean for you to get hurt."

Hunter put his hand on Quentin's. "I know. That's why you were there in the first place. Because you were looking out for me."

"I should have never followed you."

"And I should have never gone in the first place. We can play this game all night. What's done is done."

"You're being awfully forgiving."

"Yeah, well, my head hurts, I have drugs in my system, and I'm hungry."

Quentin jumped up from his chair. "Oh shit. The doctor said you're supposed to feed."

Hunter had actually meant for food—a juicy cheeseburger and salty fries sounded delicious right about now—but he wasn't going to say no to Quentin's blood.

"I should probably tell you that Dante is here."

"Fuck." He hadn't really thought what being in the clinic meant. Of course, the leader of the Guardians would be called. He was so screwed.

"Yeah. Both he and Damien know about the fighting. I couldn't keep it from Damien when I couldn't wake you up."

"No, I get it. What did you tell them?"

"Not much yet. I didn't…" Quentin took a deep breath. "I didn't want to leave your side until you woke up."

Hunter smiled at that despite knowing he was probably going to get in trouble.

"Anyway, Dante was in here when the doctor said you needed to feed when you woke up, and he offered to do it and—"

"And you want me to drink from him." If Hunter had thought his head hurt before, it was nothing compared to the pain in his chest.

Quentin nervously rubbed the back of his neck. "Uh...no..."

"What is it then?"

"Never mind." Quentin dropped his arm and pointed his thumb toward the door. "If you'd rather I go and get him, I can. He is a vampire after all. And I'm not."

"Do you want to feed me?"

Quentin laughed uncertainly, almost at some joke Hunter wasn't privy to. "Yes."

"Then, get over here."

Quentin sat on the edge of Hunter's bed. "It wasn't my place to claim the right to feed you, but I'm sure glad I get to."

Hunter's brow furrowed in confusion. Quentin's wording was odd, but maybe Hunter misunderstood. Besides, he didn't care because he was going to get to put his mouth on Quentin's skin and drink from him. "Take off your shirt."

Quentin glanced toward the door. "Are you sure that's wise? I know how you feel about getting caught."

He smiled. Maybe he should be drugged up more often because, right now, he didn't care if the king and queen walked in on him feeding from Quentin. Hunter shrugged. "It's a vampire clinic. I think everyone who's here has seen others being fed."

Quentin pulled off his shirt, and Hunter was about to tell him he didn't really have to do that. Hunter could drink from his wrist just as easily. But he stopped when he saw all of

Quentin's gorgeous, dark skin and muscle and decided to enjoy a half-naked Quentin.

"You're beautiful," he said with a sigh.

Quentin lifted an eyebrow. "I think you're right about being drugged, but I'm not going to complain."

"Lie down beside me."

Quentin turned to the door again.

"Fuck them. Lie down, so I don't hurt my head while feeding."

Quentin smiled. "Whatever you say." He swung his legs up on the bed and lay down, so he was face-to-face with Hunter.

"I like the sound of that. Take off the rest of your clothes, so I can admire your whole body."

"No. Even I'm not comfortable with that in a clinic room."

THIRTY-TWO

"YOU'RE NO FUN."

Quentin laughed at Hunter. He hated to admit that he liked seeing the vampire on meds. This was how Hunter should always be. He was usually too wound up and worried about everything.

Quentin gently put his hand on the back of Hunter's head and urged him forward. "Come on. Drink."

As much as he liked it when Hunter fed from him, Quentin was worried someone would walk in and start asking questions. He might hate that Hunter was in the closet, but he respected Hunter's decision. And he wasn't going to have Hunter regret getting caught once he was sober.

Hunter nuzzled Quentin's neck with his nose and licked him. Quentin sighed as Hunter sucked on his skin and then groaned when his teeth pierced Quentin flesh.

He was already hard. There was something about knowing his blood was making Hunter stronger and healthier. It was the ultimate aphrodisiac.

He tried to keep his erection away from the vampire out of

regard for his health, but he couldn't push Hunter away when he began rubbing his dick against his own.

By the time Hunter finished feeding, the two of them were breathing hard, and the air smelled of their arousal.

Hunter ran his hand down Quentin's chest. "Fuck. I can feel how much you want me through your blood." He pushed his pelvis into Quentin's. "I want you to fuck me."

Quentin groaned. "I want to feel what you feel. It must be amazing."

Hunter grinned a little slyly.

"What are you thinking?"

Hunter picked up Quentin's hand. "Can you shift just your hand so that your claw comes out?"

"You mean, like this?"

Within seconds, Hunter was holding the paw of a wolf.

"That is so badass."

Quentin chuckled. "I guess."

Hunter ran his finger under the tip of one claw. "Damn, that's sharp."

"How else am I supposed to catch my prey?"

Hunter met his eyes. "You just smile at them and crook your finger."

Quentin sucked in a breath. "I meant, food."

Hunter lifted his head and kissed Quentin. "I didn't." He lay back down and put his finger over Quentin's paw.

Quentin watched in fascination as Hunter brought his paw to his throat and used a claw to cut his neck. It was small and not that deep. Hunter wasn't going to bleed out or anything, but Quentin immediately shifted and jerked his hand away.

"What the hell are you doing?"

Hunter grabbed the back of Quentin's head and brought it down to his neck. "Drink, Quentin, before my blood goes to waste."

Hunter had seemed to anticipate what Quentin's argument

was going to be, and he had a point. He should grab a towel to place on Hunter's neck, but he was too curious. And the smell. Hunter's blood smelled sweet.

Quentin tentatively stuck out his tongue and licked the drop rolling down Hunter's clavicle. His blood tasted sweet, too, and Quentin wanted more.

Hunter moaned. "More. I've never fed someone like this before."

Quentin wasn't sure what he meant, except that he was somehow special and that was all the encouragement he needed.

He wrapped his mouth around Hunter's wound and sucked.

Bam.

It went straight to his groin, and Quentin almost came in his pants.

"Fuck, yes, Quentin, don't stop." Hunter grabbed the front of Quentin's pants and made quick work of his button and zipper. Hunter's finger brushed against his dick.

Quentin whimpered and started to pull away. Hunter slammed his hand down on the back of Quentin's head.

Message received. *Don't stop drinking.*

Quentin ran his hand down the front of Hunter's gown and began yanking on it to bring it up, so he could at least touch Hunter's dick. He was pretty sure he'd read that orgasms were good for one's health, so getting Hunter off would help him recover.

Or so Quentin told himself.

But Hunter batted his hand away.

Fucking alpha male. Quentin wanted to play. But the fight for dominance only made him hotter. He might as well face the fact that he was going to come all over Hunter's hospital bed.

But that was what clean sheets were for.

Except he didn't have to worry about that because Hunter

hooked his leg over Quentin's and pushed himself down onto Quentin's length.

He had no idea where Hunter had gotten the lube, but he was eternally grateful. Hunter was slick and tight, and Quentin bucked his hips, trying to get further inside Hunter's ass.

Quentin grunted, keeping his mouth on Hunter as the vampire dragged his hand down Quentin's bare back.

"Shh," Hunter said. "I got you." He slipped his hand underneath Quentin's pants and underwear, which were halfway off his ass, and squeezed.

Quentin moaned. He liked that.

"Are you going to come soon?"

Quentin nodded.

"Good," Hunter whispered and slipped a greased-up finger right in Quentin's asshole. Two thrusts, and Hunter hit the right spot.

Quentin curled back his lips and bit down on Hunter as he came in a roaring rush. He held on to Hunter with an iron grip, and he felt his nails dig into the vampire's back. But still, didn't let go until he was nothing but a quivering pile of flesh.

Hunter withdrew his finger and slid his leg off of Quentin's hip.

Quentin jerked as his still-hard and knotted dick reluctantly departed Hunter's body.

That was the best orgasm Quentin had ever had. So much so that he realized that he still had his teeth in Hunter's shoulder.

Carefully unlocking his jaw, he pulled away from Hunter and winced.

There was no mistaking the huge wolf mating mark on the vampire. Because that was what it was to Quentin. And he suddenly didn't care if they had to stay a secret. He wanted Hunter to be his.

Quentin met Hunter's blissed-out eyes as the vampire

rolled onto his back and knew that now was not the time to talk about the two of them being together. He needed Hunter to be of sound mind and body. Not fresh from surgery and high from both medication and an orgasm.

At least, he hoped that look was from coming.

Quentin looked down and saw that Hunter had climaxed all over his own belly. And suddenly, he wanted to be the one to clean him up.

Quentin moved down Hunter's body and kissed the vampire's hip.

Hunter put his hand on Quentin's head and kneaded it.

Quentin sucked the opposite hip before lapping up Hunter's cum. He continued to lick Hunter's abdomen, enjoying the sounds he made and the way his muscles tensed. When his belly was clear, Quentin ever so slowly wrapped his mouth around Hunter's dick, which was hardening again, and cleaned him off there too.

Quentin had only meant to suck away all evidence that they'd had sex, but when Hunter's breathing increased and he started thrusting his hips, Quentin kept his mouth on Hunter. He lifted one of Hunter's legs and pushed two fingers into his hole.

Hunter was still slick from the lube and from Quentin's own cum. He went straight for Hunter's prostate and rubbed until he came down Quentin's throat. He didn't know if it was his imagination, but he swore Hunter's cum tasted sweet, just like his blood.

THIRTY-THREE

QUENTIN GOT up from Hunter's hospital bed, found a washcloth, and used it to clean Hunter's ass. He didn't want the vampire to have to lie in a puddle of semen. He lowered Hunter's gown, pulled up the blankets, and then used another clean cloth to carefully wash away any blood left on Hunter's neck.

Hunter reached out and touched Quentin's cheek as he was being taken care of.

Quentin pulled up the gown as high as he could and tied it in the back.

Hunter pushed his fingers between Quentin's eyebrows. "What's wrong?"

Quentin smiled wearily. "Do you have a vampire friend who can keep a secret?"

"I think so. Why?"

"Because I bit you awfully hard and your hospital gown doesn't quite cover it. You should maybe have someone come and heal it."

Hunter smiled and touched his neck. "I guess I could call Ram."

Quentin immediately saw red, and he growled low and deep.

Hunter laughed. *Laughed*. "Okay, so I won't call Ram." He pushed Quentin in the chest. "Stop growling. It was your idea."

Quentin took a few calming breaths. "Do you have any female or mated male friends you could call?" he asked while trying to use a level voice.

"Nah. I like it."

"Hunter."

He put his hand on Quentin's and met his eyes. "I said, I like it."

And just like that, a strange sensation of pride washed over Quentin, but it wasn't his emotion.

Quentin gasped as he realized that he could sense Hunter's pride in wearing his mark.

"Is this what you feel from me all the time?"

Hunter smiled. "Nah. You're a pretty good blocker. And this is me being wide open with you."

"It's amazing." He could now sense Hunter's amusement. The emotion was like his own yet not. It was the oddest thing.

But just like that, it was gone, and Quentin was disappointed.

Hunter laughed. "I'll let you feel me again, but right now, you should probably bring Damien and Dante in here. If we take much longer, they're going to wonder why I haven't woken up yet."

That was a pretty lucid statement. Maybe Hunter wasn't as drugged up as Quentin had thought he was.

"You're probably right." He lifted his nose to the air and inhaled. "How bad do you think it smells like sex in here?" He looked at Hunter. "Are you sure you want me to let them in?"

Quentin hadn't even told Hunter yet how he'd shoved his leader against the wall. Dante already had to question why

Quentin was being so possessive. If he came in here now, he'd know for sure that he and Hunter were involved.

"Can you help me up?"

Quentin took Hunter's hand and eased him into a sitting position. "You sure didn't need much help when you shoved a finger in my ass or my dick in yours."

Hunter laughed as he set his feet on the floor. "That's because I was lying down. I wasn't worried I'd get dizzy."

Quentin forgot about teasing Hunter and was concerned for him all over again. "And did you?"

"Just a bit. But that could be because I'm hungry."

Quentin had fucked up again. He'd fed Hunter, but how much blood had Quentin taken back from him?

"Stop worrying. I'm hungry for *food*. I haven't eaten for almost twenty-four hours."

"Oh shit. Can I get you something?"

"We'd better ask the doctor first."

"Right, right." Quentin tilted his head. "Say. I'm curious as to where you learned to do the finger thing?" He might have underestimated how much experience Hunter had gotten while he was out of the country. And while he tried not to be jealous, thinking about him with other men, it was hard not to feel possessive.

"The finger thing?" Hunter grinned. "Oh. In your ass?"

"Yeah. That one. You know I'm not generally a receiver."

Hunter wiggled his eyebrows. "Yeah, but there are straight guys who even like a digit or two in the back door."

Quentin chuckled. "Okay. True. But you still didn't know if I would like it."

Hunter shrugged. "We wouldn't know unless we tried. And now, we know. I won't do it again."

Quentin cleared his throat. "Well, I wasn't exactly saying that."

Hunter smirked. "So, you did like it. Maybe you'll even let

me top you sometime." He turned his gaze away and looked down at the bed.

Quentin held his breath and almost had to take a step back. He didn't like to bottom, but the image of Hunter riding him almost made him light-headed.

He quickly shut down that thought before Hunter picked up on what he was thinking about. They didn't have time for sex again.

"Where did you get the lube anyway?"

Hunter grinned. "It's a hospital. There's all sorts of stuff you can find to use. Like petroleum jelly." He pointed to the table next to his bed. "They give every patient a tube."

"Nice. You should probably take that home with you when you leave." Quentin lifted a shoulder. "You know, in case you need it again."

Hunter laughed. He slowly pushed himself to his feet and seemed to hold his breath as he did so, but Quentin didn't notice any wincing or swaying, so that was a good sign.

"What are you going to do?" Quentin asked now that Hunter was standing.

"Take a piss and a shower."

"But—"

"I won't get my head wet." Hunter wrapped his hand around the back of Quentin's neck and kissed him. "If you don't want to smell like a vampire, you might want to take a shower, too."

"If we do that, I think it'll take even longer for us to get Damien and Dante."

Hunter grinned. "That's probably why it's smarter for us to take turns."

"Right." Smarter but not nearly as much fun. "I'll go first."

THIRTY-FOUR

ELDON HUNG up the phone with his captain just as Quentin walked into the waiting room. Eldon breathed a sigh of relief.

Truth be told, he was feeling a little awkward, waiting around the vampire clinic, because he didn't know Hunter or any of the others that well. But he would have also felt rude, just taking off without saying something to Quentin.

And he had to admit, part of him didn't want to leave Kendall yet. But he didn't want her thinking he just wanted to be around her because they needed to finish their discussion about the baby.

"Hunter is awake," Quentin announced. "And while he's a little loopy from the anesthesia or pain meds, he seems to have all his faculties about him. He's even taking a shower at the moment."

The waiting room, which was filled with vampires and shifters, erupted in cheers.

Quentin actually looked surprised at their reactions.

"Hunter's been living with us for over a year now," the wolf-shifter named Chase said. "He's like family."

Quentin smiled. "I'm sure he'll be glad to know you are all

worried about him." His look became serious as he turned to Damien and a big, hulking vampire Eldon had never seen before. "Damien, Dante, Hunter and I are ready to talk to you."

Dante. He was the leader of the Guardians. That made sense he was here, given what little Eldon knew—which was that, as of that morning, when he'd spoken to Quentin at the station, neither of their leaders had been told about the fighting. But now, with the issue with Hunter, they both were about to find out in a bad way.

The two leaders went through the double doors.

"Quentin," Eldon called out before he was gone, too.

The wolf stopped and waited.

"I'm glad that your friend is doing okay."

"Thanks. Me, too. Thank you for helping us get him here."

"To protect and serve, am I right?"

Quentin smiled. "You're right."

"Anyway, I wanted to touch base with you before I took off. We can meet up again in a few days when your friend is better, and we can discuss where to go from there. The fighting ring isn't going anywhere."

"Thank you. I honestly forgot to even tell Hunter about meeting with you today."

"Hey, it's okay. I understand you had more pressing things on your mind."

Quentin nodded. "I did. I do." He met Eldon's eyes. "But I want you to know, I'm with you one hundred percent. It's because of this fighting ring that Hunter got hurt, and I can't imagine he's the first. It needs to be shut down. It's a bunch of amateurs without any training or equipment. Someone is going to end up dead if we don't stop them."

"I'm glad to hear that."

That fire that burned in Quentin's belly was the kind of determination Eldon needed to get the job done. Other detectives might see it as a liability, but Eldon trusted him. He was a sentinel and a shifter. Quentin would do the right thing when it came down to it.

"You have my number?"

"I do."

He slapped Quentin on the shoulder. "We'll talk soon."

Eldon watched Quentin walk through the doors and sighed. It was time to talk to Kendall again. But now that a lot of his initial anger had subsided, he didn't have a clue as to what to say to her.

☾

Kendall stared at Eldon as he came toward her.

"Hey. I was wondering if we could finish our conversation. Now that we know Hunter is okay."

She looked at Raven, who nodded. Kendall had filled her in while they were waiting to hear about Hunter.

She nodded and went to push herself up from the chair when Eldon took her hands and helped her stand. It was such a simple gesture, but now, she knew why she hadn't told him about the baby.

She'd told herself it was because she didn't want to make his life complicated and that they needed to stay away from each other because of what had happened with his brother, but those were minor excuses.

The real reason was that it'd made her realize how very alone she was. It was one thing to be alone and a single mom because she chose to be. It was another thing when it was forced upon her.

But she didn't want to be alone.

She knew enough about Eldon to know he would do right by the baby. She'd seen his chivalrous side, and it wasn't weak.

She didn't know if a relationship with Eldon was right, but she'd like to try.

As crazy as it sounded, one of the reasons she hadn't told him was because she liked him. If she didn't, she probably would have told him right away, not caring if he decided not to be a part of her life.

"You okay?" he asked her.

Oh crap. She'd zoned out. "Yeah, I'm fine. Is your car still at our place?"

Eldon had arrived in the vehicle that brought Hunter to the clinic in case he was needed, and she had driven separately.

"Yes."

"Come on. I'll take you there. We can talk in the car."

They walked silently out to the parking lot, and she led Eldon to her car. She studied him as they went. He had dark hair with blue eyes, and he was tall and attractive. When she'd first seen him tonight, he'd been wearing a full suit, but now, he was missing his jacket, and the sleeves of his dress shirt were rolled up to show off his muscular forearms.

He wasn't as big or jacked as most of the males she lived with, but she'd seen him naked, and she knew he had to work out. It made sense he would stay in shape for his job, and she certainly wasn't going to complain.

She had often wondered if she had been attracted to him simply because of her heat, but she could now confirm that wasn't true.

It was crazy, but she might even be more attracted to him now.

They reached her car, and she sighed at the thought of getting behind the wheel.

"Do you want me to drive?" Eldon asked, reading her mind.

"Do you mind? I prefer not driving nowadays."

"Not at all."

She handed him the keys and waddled over to the passenger side.

As they drove back to her home, she waited for Eldon to start a conversation with her since he had indicated he wanted to talk. But so far, they'd ridden in ever-increasing uncomfortable silence.

"Do you hate me?" she blurted out.

Eldon jerked the wheel and swung his head in her direction and looked at her like she was crazy. "*What?*"

"Do you hate me? For not telling you about the baby?"

"No, I don't hate you."

That was a relief. Kind of.

"But you're mad at me."

"I'm not mad exactly. I'm upset." He glanced her way. "I'm disappointed."

Yikes. That wasn't good.

She squeezed her hands together. "I don't blame you."

"Would you have told me?"

"Yes."

He gave her a quick raised eyebrow.

"Eventually," she admitted.

"And what is *eventually*? When the baby went to college?"

"*No.* More like when I was in labor, so you'd have to be nice to me, no matter what, because I was going to give birth."

Eldon laughed. That was a good sign. She hoped.

"Honestly, I'm sad that I already missed so much." He looked at her belly. "You're in your third trimester. I've missed everything with the first two. And it makes me sad to think about what else I might have missed if I hadn't come to your house."

Guilt settled on her shoulders like a heavy weight. If the situation were reversed, she'd feel the same way. Honestly, she might not be as nice as Eldon was being about it.

When they pulled up to the house, Eldon parked near his SUV.

"Will you come upstairs to my room before you go? Please?"

He nodded, and she released the large breath she'd been holding.

They exited the vehicle and entered the empty house.

She led the way up the stairs, not bothering to turn on the lights. She opened the door to her room. "Come in. Sit on the bed, please."

Eldon raised his brow but didn't ask what she was up to.

She turned on the lamp on her dresser and another by her bed. She was about to do something that was going to take a lot of courage, and she didn't know if she could do it under the bright overhead light.

She clasped her hands in front of her. "I can't help you gain back the stuff you lost by me not telling you right away or even when it was safe to see you again. I have no idea what things would have been like from your side, but I can share what it's been like for me."

She took a deep breath.

"The first trimester was pretty uneventful. I found out right before you earned your commendation from the police department. Congratulations, by the way. I didn't have any morning sickness, but I did sleep and pee a lot."

The corner of Eldon's mouth lifted, and she took it as a good sign that he appreciated her peace offering.

"The beginning of my second trimester wasn't much different. My belly started growing, but it was very small at first, of course. The worst part was finding clothes to wear because I wasn't big enough for maternity clothes, but none of my pants or shorts fit. I wasn't sick in the first trimester, but I got quite the appetite in the second." She chuckled. "I still do actually."

This gained her a full smile from Eldon, so she kept going,

"Which leads us to now. I only just started my third trimester a few weeks ago, but it's getting harder for me to breathe, and even though I like to eat, I don't have as much room in my stomach."

She squeezed her eyes shut and told herself she could do the next part. No matter what, Eldon wouldn't laugh at her.

Before she second-guessed herself, she pulled her shirt over her head, kicked off her pants, and removed her bra and panties until she was naked.

THIRTY-FIVE

KENDALL STARED in Eldon's direction but tried to avoid eye contact, afraid of what she would see on his face. Her biggest fear was disgust because it wasn't just that she had gained weight.

But that was why she was doing this. If she could bare herself to him—literally and figuratively—hopefully, he would know how truly sorry she was for not including him sooner.

She stepped closer so that she was looking down on him. That way, she wouldn't have to meet his eyes.

She cupped her breasts. "My boobs have gotten bigger, and so have my areolas. I feel like they're the size of dinner plates," she said, laughing nervously.

She ran her hands down to her abdomen and traced the jagged white lines. "As much as I tried to avoid them, I have stretch marks. It's funny because they look painful, but they don't hurt. They're just ugly."

She widened her legs. "I won't subject you to actually looking at my crotch." She laughed, hoping he would, too. "I haven't trimmed in months. It's too hard." She glanced down at her feet. "And I can barely tie my own shoes. I've been utilizing my slip-on collection."

She lessened her stance and pointed out her last flaw. "I've also been slacking on shaving my legs. If it wasn't for them bothering me while I slept, I would let them go completely, too. Right now, I'm about three days out."

There had to be something else she could share with him that was embarrassing. Her conversation with Raven from that morning came back to her.

"Oh, and I haven't had sex in forever." She turned her gaze down at her stomach. "Seven months, to be exact." She laughed. "And while I was okay with it in the beginning because I was tired all the time, lately, I've been super horny. It sucks. Not only do I not want to go out and find some rando while pregnant, but who would want me anyway? Minus the pregnancy fetish guys. No, thank you."

Eldon lifted his head and met her eyes.

She couldn't read his expression, and she hoped she hadn't messed up. She shrugged. "Well, that's all I can think of right now."

She went to take a step back, but Eldon grabbed her hand.

"Yes?" she asked.

"If this is too forward, I give you permission to smack me."

She smiled. "Okay."

He met her eyes. "Can I touch you?"

She lifted her arms. "I'm all yours."

A tiny smile crossed his lips, and she blushed. She just now caught the sexual innuendo. She hadn't meant it at the time, but now, she did.

She cut off all thoughts of sex because she didn't want him to feel like he was obligated to have sex with her just because she'd taken her clothes off. That hadn't been her intention.

Although it sure would be nice.

"I'm going to touch your belly."

"It's okay," she encouraged him. "I'll let you know if I get uncomfortable."

"Thank you," he said, appearing relieved. He moved his eyes down to her stomach and began running his hands over her. "It's..."

"So hard?"

"Yeah."

"I know. For some reason, I always thought a pregnant belly would be soft. It was firm right from the beginning. Sorry, I guess I forgot that tidbit."

"I'm going to touch your breasts now."

She swallowed. "Okay."

Eldon cupped her breasts in his hands and ran his thumbs around the outsides of her areolas. He circled her nipples, getting closer with each pass. By the time he reached the inside, she was holding her breath, worried he'd stop.

His thumbs brushed over her now-stiff peaks, and she moaned as the scent of her arousal filled her bedroom. His hands on her shouldn't feel that good.

Eldon's hands moved down from her breasts to her back where they stopped at her hips. He pulled her between his legs and looked up at her face. "I'm going to taste them now."

Her lips parted as she drew in a shallow breath. She practically whimpered when he sucked a nipple into her mouth. The air was now heavy with her scent, and she was so wet that a drop rolled down the inside of her thigh.

Eldon lifted his mouth from her chest and licked his lips. "I can taste you."

Kendall gasped in mortification. She'd read that she could start leaking colostrum during the third trimester, but she hadn't seen any evidence of it yet.

Her face heated so quickly that she felt like she might pass out.

Eldon stood, so their bodies touched. He took one hand

from her hip and lifted her chin. "Don't be embarrassed. It's perfectly natural."

"I would have warned you if I had known. I swear it's never happened before."

He smiled sweetly. "It's okay. I happen to think it's cool as hell."

He bent his head and pressed his lips to hers. He flicked his tongue against the seam of her mouth, and she opened for him. He deepened their kiss, and she soon forgot all about her humiliation.

Eldon dragged his hand up and cupped her breast again, squeezing her nipple. He kissed down her neck and pulled the pink bud into his mouth.

Kendall wrapped her arms around his neck and moaned. She got the message. He didn't think she was gross.

As he kissed her again, his hand traveled south and skimmed her curls. He picked up her leg and set her foot on the bed as he raised his head. "I'm going to touch your pussy now."

"Oh, yes, please," she said breathlessly.

His hand slipped between her legs, and when he slid two fingers inside her and brushed his thumb over her clit, she almost exploded.

But Eldon took his hand away from her all too fast. He'd touched her for less than five minutes.

He carefully nudged her, and her leg fell from the bed as Eldon pushed her a few steps back.

She was ready to fight him for an orgasm when she saw he was unbuttoning his shirt. She watched as it slowly opened, and she sighed at the sight of his bare chest. Amazingly, she was even more aroused now.

Next, Eldon undid his dress pants and pushed them off his hips. She saw his sexy V first but soon forgot about it when his cock burst forth, looking proud and hard.

She licked her lips. She'd never had her mouth there, but she'd bet he tasted as good as he looked.

Eldon lifted her chin again as he sat back down on her bed and drew her toward him. He continued to pull her until she had a knee on each side of him.

"I want you to put me inside you. But only if you're okay with that."

Kendall enveloped his head in her arms and kissed him. Gradually, she lowered her wet core over his shaft, but she had to break their kiss, so she could breathe. She dropped her forehead to his and held on tight as his cock stretched her open.

Her pussy was already contracting by the time he was fully inside her. She wasn't going to last long.

He splayed his hand across her back. "Ride me. I'm all yours."

Steadily, she started rocking her hips, increasing her speed as she continued. She soon was crying out as her orgasm neared, and she wished she could remember if he'd always felt this good inside her.

Her eyes were squeezed shut when Eldon said her name, "Kendall."

She opened her lids and met his gaze.

"I'm going to make you come now."

He pressed a thumb against her clit, and she ignited, her orgasm taking such full control of her body that she could no longer hang on.

She vaguely acknowledged Eldon picking her up and laying her across her bed. Taking her hands in his, he raised them over her head and pounded into her. She was barely finished with her climax when the second one hit her almost as strongly as the first.

"Oh my God, Eldon," she called out as she gripped him with her inner muscles.

"Almost there with you." Eldon slammed into her two more

times and exploded inside her. His seed was so hot that she could feel it.

As soon as his barbs receded, he pulled out and lay down beside her, keeping one of her hands in his.

She bent her knees to take the pressure off her back and felt Eldon's cum slide out of her. "I think I needed that."

Eldon chuckled. "You weren't lying when you said you were horny."

Her eyes drifted closed. "No, I wasn't. And now, I'm sated and tired."

She felt Eldon move beside her, and she opened her eyes to see him leaning over her.

"I didn't hurt you, did I? Or the baby?"

"We're both great."

He ran a hand over her belly and was rewarded with a kick.

"See? We're both fine."

Eldon kissed her on the lips. "Let me tuck you in."

She pushed a lock of dark hair off his forehead. "Do you forgive me for not telling you sooner?"

He smiled. "Yes. I could never stay upset with you for long."

"In that case, yes, you can tuck me in. On one condition."

"What's that?"

"That you tuck yourself in right along with me."

THIRTY-SIX

THE FOLLOWING NIGHT, Quentin helped Hunter into the house. Actually, it was more like Hunter let Quentin help him into the house. Hunter's limbs worked just fine, and he didn't need Quentin to hold his elbow on the stairs.

"You know they did surgery on my head, right?" Hunter asked as he stopped on the porch stairs.

"Yes, I'm well aware."

"Then, you know I can walk on my own."

"I don't want you to get dizzy and fall, asshole."

Hunter laughed and leaned over to kiss Quentin on the lips but stopped short when the door opened, and Damien stepped out.

He wished he had the courage to kiss Quentin, no matter who was around.

"Hey, Hunter. How are you feeling?" Damien asked.

"Good. Thank you for asking." Hunter grabbed the railing and continued heading up. He forgot to ask Quentin if Damien was still upset at the two of them today.

Last night, Damien and Dante had been pretty pissed at both Hunter and Quentin for going to the fights. Hunter defended Quentin because he'd only been there to make sure Hunter was safe. But Damien had pointed out that Quentin still should have alerted Damien and taken backup.

Dante had wanted Hunter to come back to stay with the vampires, but Hunter had insisted on staying with the wolf-shifters. If he was going to be of any help with the investigation, it made sense for him to be close to Quentin.

Plus, he simply wanted to be close to Quentin.

"I'll get Eldon," Damien said.

"He's already here?" Quentin asked even though Damien had gone back inside.

After Hunter and Quentin's incredible sex session at the hospital, Hunter had been *this close* to saying to hell with his job and life so long as he got to be with Quentin. But part of him had known it was the drugs talking. He honestly didn't know what his life would be like if he was no longer a sentinel.

He didn't know where he'd live or what he'd do for work. And he had no idea how his parents—two very traditional vampires in their thinking—would feel about him being gay. They probably wouldn't let him move back home with them.

Gay, homeless, and jobless. They'd never understand him giving up everything like that to be with some wolf.

In a way, Hunter almost had to stay in the closet to be with Quentin.

How fucked up is that?

Hunter shrugged. "He must be."

"Hey," Quentin asked once they were in the house, "are you okay?"

"Yeah. Why?"

His brow was furrowed in concern. "You look...sad all of a sudden."

Hunter forced a smile. "I'm fine."

"You sure?"

Not really. "Yep."

Damien came downstairs with Eldon right then.

Hunter leaned toward Quentin and whispered, "What was the police detective doing upstairs?"

"Kendall finally told him about the baby."

Hunter leaned back as his eyes widened. "Really?"

Quentin laughed and nodded his head. "More like he accidentally found out, but yes."

"Wow."

"Yeah. And it looks and smells like he's just fine with the pregnancy."

Hunter understood exactly what Quentin meant. The cat-shifter smelled like Kendall and sex. "I agree."

Quentin burst out laughing but still managed to hold out his hand to the detective when he approached. "Hello again."

The cat-shifter shook Quentin's hand. "Hello."

"This is Hunter, the one I was telling you about at the station. Hunter, this is Detective Conrad."

Hunter shook hands with the male.

"You can call me Eldon." He looked at Quentin. "You, too. We're not at work." He turned back to Hunter. "And I'm glad to see that you're doing better."

Without thinking about it, Hunter patted the bald spot on the back of his head where they had cut him open. "Thanks. I'm glad to be home."

Eldon put his hands on his hips. "Should we sit and discuss the plan?"

"Let's do it," Quentin said.

"I'm ready," Hunter agreed.

Damien led them to his office, and they all sat.

Eldon started, "I don't know how much Quentin has told you, Hunter, but I would like to bring you in as a confidential informant." He stood, grabbed a folder off of Damien's desk, and handed it to Hunter. "This is the paperwork I need you to fill out. This will get you on the books. When do you think you can have it back to me?"

It hurt Hunter's head to read small print for very long. He'd given up on his discharge papers after the first page. But he didn't want to keep Eldon waiting.

"I'll help him with it tonight," Quentin said.

"Perfect," Eldon said. "Next, can you tell me what you know and how you got involved?"

Hunter crafted his words carefully. He didn't want to let on that it had all started because he was jealous of Quentin being with another man.

"I was at a bar, and someone tried to pick a fight with me." Hunter held up his hands. "And I admit that I really wanted to punch the smart mouth off of him. But I knew it would end badly. Apparently, Trey had been watching the whole thing. He's the guy who approached me. He sat down at my table and told me there was a place I could fight without getting in any trouble."

"What's Trey's full name?" Eldon asked just as Quentin said, "Why did you want to fight?"

Hunter ignored Quentin. "Trey is all I know. He never gave me his last name. But I have a phone number." Hunter took out his phone, found the number, and handed it over to Eldon. "Here you go."

"Why didn't I meet Trey?" Quentin asked, a scowl on his face.

Hunter shrugged. "I don't know. He wasn't there that night. He did give me the location though."

"I see that," Eldon said, shaking Hunter's phone. "So, you have never communicated with Tank or Wayne through phone calls or texts?"

Hunter shook his head. "No."

Eldon rubbed his chin. "Then, I think the first goal will be to get their phone numbers, so we can try to track them. If we can find out where they go or who they talk to, it might lead us to some bigger players. Since Trey wasn't at the last fight, you can use that as an excuse to ask them—like, what happens if Trey doesn't answer and you want to fight? That should be enough of a reason to get their information."

"But Hunter can't fight," Quentin said.

Eldon smiled. "He can't fight right now, but this investigation isn't going to be finished overnight. This isn't a movie. It's going to be slow and sometimes boring. Until then, you can fight. And Hunter can place bets. If they're making money off you two, I don't think they'll care how they do it." He pointed his finger at Hunter. "But don't tell them that the fighting injury sent you to the clinic. They might think you want revenge. And don't lose every bet you make. It'll start to look suspicious. But don't win them all either, or they won't want you to come back."

Hunter nodded. "Got it."

"I think that's about it for now. We'll meet up again after you go to a fight." Eldon looked at his watch. "When is the next fight anyway?"

"I'm sure there's one tonight," Hunter answered.

Quentin stood and swiped his hands out. "No. No way. You cannot go tonight. You need to rest. I don't know if you should even go tomorrow night." Fast healer or not, Quentin wasn't sure twenty-four hours would be enough time for Hunter to improve.

Eldon smiled at Quentin's concern. "I wasn't suggesting Hunter go tonight. Even if Hunter was up for it, those guys would take one look at him and tell him to take a hike. They wouldn't want him dying on their watch. They're trying to avoid the police, remember?" He patted Hunter's shoulder. "You rest tonight, and we'll see how you feel tomorrow. If you're not ready, we can wait. Okay?"

"Okay."

"Any questions, Damien?" Eldon asked.

"Nope. This is your operation. As long as my guys are protected, I'm fine with whatever you decide."

"We'll talk again tomorrow," Eldon said, standing. "But right now, I have to go and make up for lost time."

THIRTY-SEVEN

TUESDAY AFTERNOON, Raven walked into the after-school center. She hadn't communicated with Monica since Saturday night, and even though things seemed fine, Raven had a feeling that everything was not okay.

Not wanting to come on too strongly, Raven went about her normal business and waited for Monica to approach her.

But Monica had been holed up in her office since Raven arrived, and there were no signs of her coming out.

"I haven't seen Monica at all. Is that normal?" she asked another volunteer.

"Sometimes," he answered. "If she has a lot of paperwork or something."

It made sense, but why wouldn't Monica just do the paperwork when the students weren't there? But there was no way to know the truth until she went and knocked on the door.

But Raven didn't have to do that because, a few minutes later, Monica came out.

"Hey."

Monica smiled at her, and as far as Raven could tell, it looked sincere. "Hey, Raven."

"How was the rest of the weekend?"

"Good. Sorry we lost each other on Friday."

"That's okay. It's not the first time it's happened, and I'm sure it won't be the last. I feel bad we didn't say good-bye."

Monica waved away Raven's concern. "It's fine. I'm a big girl. I can take care of myself." Her attention was drawn away from Raven to the entrance.

Raven followed her gaze to see a large male walking toward them. She had never seen him before.

"I need to go," Monica said. "We'll talk later, Raven."

"Okay. Later."

"Francis." Monica waved at the guy to get his attention as she walked over to him.

The man scowled. "Don't call me that."

Monica grinned. "But you just love it when I do," she teased him.

"Who the heck is that?" Raven asked, thinking out loud.

"That's Frank, Monica's brother."

Raven turned around to see one of the kids standing there, and she chuckled nervously. She hadn't meant for anyone to hear her. "Thanks."

"No problem," the student said and walked away.

Raven narrowed her eyes as she remembered what the girls had talked about in the restroom the day she was eavesdropping. One of Monica's tests was to have sex with her brother.

Ignoring the queasiness in her stomach, she waited for the two siblings to go to Monica's office before she snuck over and put her ear to the door.

"How did Saturday go?" Frank asked.

"Good. The new girl had a few hiccups, but she did okay. You know how they are in the beginning—timid and scared—but they always come around."

So, that was what Monica had been doing on Saturday night. It still didn't explain though how she had been able to message Raven back if she wasn't home and her phone said it was. She really needed to have Lachlan look into this. Monica could have cloned her phone, but it wasn't Raven's area of expertise. While Raven didn't know the specifics, she was sure Lachlan did.

"How was your Saturday night?"

"We had our own little hiccup, but we figured it out."

"Are you sure?" Monica asked.

"Yes." Frank sounded a little nervous, which was funny because he was way bigger than his sister.

"Good."

"So, who am I here for today?"

"Her name is Virginia. I'm not sure about her, so no kid gloves, okay? I'm not taking her to the next party if she can't handle you."

Raven silently slammed her hand over her mouth. So, that was why Monica's brother was there.

Sick.

"You don't have to worry about me."

"We'll see. I'll go get her."

Raven spun and hurried away. She needed to find Virginia. Although this would be the perfect way to catch Monica in the act, she could not let Virginia go through with this.

Adrenaline flooded her body as she searched for the girl. "Come on, come on, come on. Where are you?"

There.

Virginia and Calli were standing in a corner. Calli had her arm around Virginia in what looked like comfort. Raven sprinted over, picking up the end of the conversation.

"It'll be okay. Just close your eyes and pretend you're somewhere else. Pretend you're spending all that money you're going to make. It'll be over before you know it."

Raven wanted to yell at Calli for encouraging her friend to

do something she didn't want to do, but Calli was just as much of a victim as Virginia was.

"Virginia. Calli."

The girls looked up when they heard Raven say their names.

"I need you to come with me."

They looked at each other.

"Now."

"Okay," Calli said. "What do you need?"

"Let's go outside." Raven checked for Monica over her shoulder. So far, there was no sign of her, but it sounded like she could be coming any minute.

Raven hustled the girls outside and away from the building, but now that she was there, she didn't know what to do next. If she disappeared with them, Monica would surely know something was up. But Raven didn't have time to call anyone else to come and get them, and they couldn't leave on their own.

Raven pulled out her keys and hit the key fob, so her lights blinked. She handed the keys to Virginia. "I need you girls to go and get in my car."

Calli looked at Raven like she was crazy. "We don't know you. You can't kidnap us."

"I'm not kidnapping you. Please, you have to trust me."

Calli crossed her arms over her chest. "No way."

This girl was the wrong one to try to reason with.

Raven turned her attention to Virginia. "Look, I know what's about to happen. And I know you don't want to go through with it. I'm here to help you."

Virginia bit her lip and looked at her friend.

"How do you know?" Calli asked.

"I just do. Now, will you two please, please go get in my car? I will explain everything later," Raven pleaded with them.

"I don't want to do it, Cal," Virginia said.

Calli went from defiant to concerned. "Okay." She

narrowed her eyes at Raven. "But if you're trying to abduct us, I will fight like hell."

Raven put her hands together like she was praying. "I'm not. Please go."

Calli snatched the keys out of Virginia's hand. "Let's go, Gin."

Raven breathed a sigh of relief and ran back into the building. Monica was looking around, but Raven kept herself out of her view.

Raven found the nearest volunteer. "Hey, I have to go. Family emergency."

The other female frowned. "Everything okay?"

"It will be. But I don't have time to tell Monica."

"That's okay. I'll do it."

"Thank you," Raven said and ran out of the center.

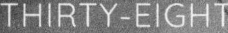

THIRTY-EIGHT

QUENTIN LOOKED up from the couch in the living room as Hunter came down the stairs. He was rubbing his eyes, and Quentin was glad to see that Hunter had slept all day. It was clear that he had just woken up, but he looked a hundred times better than he had the night before.

"What's going on?" Hunter asked, pointing to the commotion upstairs.

"Raven brought in two girls who were caught up in a prostitution ring. They're not sure what to do with them right now. They're debating on if the girls should stay the night here or go back with their parents."

"Does this have to do with Willow Clifton and the after-school program?"

"It sounds like it. I've been staying out of the way. Too many cooks in the kitchen, you know."

Hunter came to sit beside him. "Plus, we have our own thing to deal with."

Quentin cleared his throat. "Speaking of that, I was thinking I should go alone tonight."

Hunter narrowed his eyes. "I'm not staying here while you

go alone."

"I think it might be too soon." Quentin reached over and cupped the back of Hunter's head. "I don't want you to get hurt."

Hunter put his hand on top of Quentin's. "I'll be fine. I'm not going to fight, remember?"

"Oh, I'm sorry."

Quentin yanked his hand away as he and Hunter turned toward the sound of the voice.

"Jeremiah?" Quentin jumped up from the couch. He looked back at Hunter, guilt flooding his body.

"I'm sorry. Someone let me in."

Quentin ran his hand over his short hair. He needed to start shaving again. "No, it's fine."

He heard Hunter moving behind him.

"I'll just get out of your way," Hunter said. He walked over to Jeremiah and held out his hand first. "I'm Hunter."

"Jeremiah," he said, shaking Hunter's hand.

"I've heard a lot about you."

"Oh."

"I'll let you two talk."

Hunter walked past Quentin and tried to smile reassuringly, but Quentin could see the unhappiness in the vampire's eyes. He hated seeing Hunter sad.

"I didn't expect to see you today," Quentin said when it was just him and Jeremiah in the room.

"I've been trying to get ahold of you, but you weren't answering your phone, so I thought I'd come over."

"Shit, I'm sorry. Things have been kind of crazy around here. Hunter had to have emergency surgery and..." And he hadn't thought about Jeremiah once. "Do you want to come in and sit?"

"I think it's best that I don't."

"Okay." Then, why was he there? "Is there something you

need?"

Jeremiah laughed, but there was no humor. "I actually came here to tell you that I wanted to be together, but it looks like I'm too late."

Quentin slumped down in the nearest chair and dropped his head in his hands. "Ah, shit, Jeremiah. I am so sorry."

"Is Hunter the guy…"

Quentin looked up. "I…can't say."

"That's a yes then."

"Jeremiah—"

Jeremiah held up his hand. "I'm not going to say anything to anyone."

Quentin frowned. "How did you…"

"Remember the night we found that little place and had too much to drink?"

Quentin struggled to recall the night Jeremiah was referring to.

"There was the cute server who kept flirting with both of us, and we joked about taking him home."

"Oh." Quentin smiled at the memory. "Yeah, I remember. I'm pretty sure he was just flirting with us because we were American and knew we'd likely tip."

There was no obligation to tip in Switzerland, but most Americans did anyway, especially when they received good service.

"And here I thought, it was because we were so good-looking."

"Well, I'm sure that played into it, too."

Jeremiah came over and sat down across from Quentin. "You might not remember, but you told me all about a guy that you had fallen hard for, who was in the closet. You and I were sharing ex-boyfriend war stories, so I never thought about it again. Until you came to my house the other day. I've been wondering if it was the same guy."

Quentin had completely forgotten he'd told Jeremiah about Hunter. They'd had a lot to drink that night. A lot. Now, he wished he had never said anything.

"Am I wrong?" Jeremiah asked.

Quentin hesitated before shaking his head. "But please don't tell anyone. It's not his fault."

Jeremiah scowled. "I already said I wouldn't."

Quentin held up his hands. "I'm sorry. I didn't mean any offense. It's just that he has a lot to lose."

Jeremiah snorted. "Don't we all?"

Quentin was a shit. "Jeremiah, I am so sorry."

"Yeah, yeah. Can I ask why you even started a relationship with me?" The bitterness in Jeremiah's voice was palpable.

"Because I liked you."

"Just not as much as Hunter."

Quentin sighed. "It's not like that. I thought I was over him. And it was really easy to think I was when it was just you and me. I was happy." He lifted his shoulders. "But then I came back and saw him...and I realized I hadn't lost all my feelings for him."

"Even if you have to keep your relationship a secret?"

Quentin dropped his head.

"I'll take that as a yes." Jeremiah laughed again. "He must be really special for you to break the one rule you have about relationships."

He is.

Quentin lifted his eyes. "I'm—"

"Ugh. Don't tell me you're sorry again."

"But I am."

Jeremiah stood. "Whatever. I hope you and Hunter are ridiculously happy together. But I doubt that's going to happen when you can't even tell anyone you love him." And with those parting words, Jeremiah was out the door.

THIRTY-NINE

HUNTER KICKED a rock and watched it fly across the driveway until it hit the garage, feeling guilty that he wished it were hitting Jeremiah's head instead.

A noise sounded from the house, and Hunter drew back into the shadows as Jeremiah stomped onto the porch. He looked upset, and when he got in his car, he revved the engine to go down the driveway faster than he should.

A minute later, Quentin came outside. "Hunter."

Hunter walked out into the light. "I'm here." He scanned Quentin's face. "Are you okay?"

"No."

"What happened?"

"He came to tell me he wanted to still be with me."

Hunter winced. "Oh."

Quentin laughed. "Don't worry. We're not together."

That would explain the scowl and stomping when Jeremiah had left.

Hunter dared to ask, "What happened?"

"You."

"Me?"

"Yeah, you."

"What did I do?"

Quentin moved toward him. "I don't know. Let me have sex with you the same night I brought him here to meet everyone."

"Hey, it's not like I made you fuck me. I believe you were the one who turned me around and pulled down my pants."

"You're right." Quentin came closer. "But then you went to the clinic and made me completely forget all about Jeremiah."

Hunter couldn't help but smile. "You forgot about him?"

"He didn't cross my mind once."

"Poor Jeremiah."

Quentin came closer until they almost touched. "Yeah, I feel awful."

"But not awful enough to run after him."

Quentin shook his head. "I don't want him." He brushed his lips over Hunter's. "Not the way I want you."

Hunter pulled Quentin into his arms and kissed him, opening his mouth and thrusting his tongue inside. Quentin clawed at his back, and Hunter wished they were alone and naked, so he could feel Quentin push inside him.

Hunter moaned as Quentin pulled away.

"*Fuck*. This sucks. I want you so bad right now, but we need to get to the fight."

Hunter groaned in frustration. "I'm not well enough to go. I think you have to stay here and take care of me."

Quentin laughed and pushed his cock against Hunter's. "If you're well enough for me to fuck you, then you're well enough to go tonight."

Hunter wrinkled his nose. "Are you sure? Because you fucked me when I was in a hospital bed. I wasn't even well enough to come home."

Quentin grinned. "I see how you are. That was grief. I was worried and relieved you were okay. And even though I was the one inside you, you fucked me, buddy. I just lay there and let you use my body for your own pleasure." Quentin stuck out his arms and put his head to the side like he'd fallen asleep.

Hunter playfully pushed him. "Asshole."

Quentin laughed and pulled Hunter to him. He met Hunter's eyes, and his face turned serious. "I want to be with you."

"I want to be with you, too."

"No. I want to *be* with you."

Hunter's throat felt thick. "You mean, like…together?"

A warm smile filled Quentin's face. "Yes. I want you to be my boyfriend, my lover, my man, or whatever you want to call it." He put his hands on Hunter's chest. "But only if that's what you want. After all, you were the one who broke things off with me."

Hunter scoffed, "A million years ago."

"But it's true."

Hunter's happiness was short-lived. "I still can't tell anyone I'm gay, Quentin. Nothing's changed. And you don't want to—"

"Shh." Quentin put his finger on Hunter's lips. "I don't care."

"What do you mean?" Hunter was afraid to hope.

"I don't care if we have to keep our relationship a secret. I don't care if we have to sneak around. As long as I get to be with you."

Hunter's eyes felt funny, and his vision blurred.

Quentin arched his neck back. "Are you okay?"

"No." Hunter's voice was shaky.

Quentin tilted his head. "So, does that mean you don't want to be with me?" He shrugged. "I guess I'll go after Jeremiah then."

He took a step away, but Hunter grabbed him around the

arm and hauled him back. "Don't you fucking dare. You're mine."

Quentin groaned, "I fucking love the sound of that. Say it again."

"You're mine."

"Damn right I am. And you're mine."

Quentin kissed him, and there was a strong chance they would have ended up doing it outside again, but someone dropped something in the house. The noise reminded him of where they were.

Quentin put his head to Hunter's. "Ugh. We are never going to be alone."

"We were the other night."

"That was a miracle. And if you recall, it didn't last long before someone came home." He gritted his teeth. "Why don't I have an apartment like everyone else?"

"I don't know. Why don't you?"

"That was rhetorical, smart-ass," Quentin said with a laugh. "I work two jobs. It's not worth it to get an apartment."

"We could always go to a hotel."

Quentin grinned. "Just like the first time we messed around together."

"That did cross my mind."

"Let's do it. We'll message Damien after the fight and tell him we are too tired to come home." Quentin planted a peck on Hunter's lips. "You're a genius." He tugged on Hunter's shirt and slipped his hands underneath. "I cannot wait to be alone with you all night."

Hunter kissed him back. "Me either."

"We'd better go."

"Yeah," Hunter agreed.

"Did you get the location from *Trey*?" Quentin said Trey's name with a little bit of a bite.

Hunter laughed and kissed Quentin on the forehead. "Yes.

And you don't need to be jealous. I'm pretty sure Trey is straight. Besides, I only have eyes for you."

As they walked to the car, Quentin tried to hide his satisfied smile, but Hunter still saw it. He wore one of his own, knowing he was the one to put it there.

They got in Quentin's SUV and headed to the site of the fight that night. Neither of them noticed the car hiding in the trees, waiting for them to go past.

FORTY

QUENTIN PULLED up to a row of cars and put his SUV in park. He pulled out a burner phone and handed it to Hunter.

"What's this?"

"It's a burner phone. The code is 6988. We need to get Wayne's or Tank's phone number, but we're not going to use ours in case they look at it." Quentin opened up his glove compartment and threw his regular phone in there. He held it open for Hunter to do the same, and then he locked it. "You have the cash for bets?"

Hunter patted his back pocket. "Right here. I'm just not sure if I should bet on you to lose or win," he said with a grin.

"Hardy-har-har." Quentin pushed his door open. "I let you win," he retorted and got out of his SUV before Hunter could say any more.

But that didn't stop the vampire. Hunter got out of his side and said, "You wish." He came around to Quentin's side and nudged him with his hip. "It's okay that you lost to a vampire."

Quentin shot him a look. "I don't care about that."

Hunter thought about that. "You don't like that you lost to me?"

"I don't like that I lost, period."

Hunter looked like he was trying not to smile. "Aw, poor baby."

Quentin lifted his middle finger and stomped off toward the crowd.

"You get to do that later, remember?" Hunter yelled from behind him.

Quentin couldn't stop the smile that came across his face. No matter what happened tonight, he was going to be alone with Hunter, and he couldn't wait.

☾

Jeremiah sat in his car on the far end of the row where Quentin and Hunter had parked and watched the two of them walk in the opposite direction of him.

He had no idea where he was or what he was doing there. And a voice inside him told him to turn around and go home.

But he couldn't get rid of the image of Quentin with his hand on Hunter when they'd thought they were alone. It had clearly been intimate. Quentin had never looked at Jeremiah like that in all the months they hung out. Not even close.

Quentin might not know it, but he was in love with Hunter. And after connecting the man on the couch to the guy Quentin had complained about back in the restaurant in Switzerland, Jeremiah was pretty sure Quentin had been in love with Hunter the whole time.

No wonder Quentin hadn't wanted to fully commit to Jeremiah.

And, boy, did that piss him off.

But he didn't blame Quentin. Quentin had tried to move on, and Jeremiah didn't think Quentin had fully meant to hurt him.

No, his anger was for fucking Hunter. If that asshole had

manned up and come out of the closet, then Quentin would never have started a relationship with Jeremiah.

On that thought, Jeremiah swung open his door and got out of his car. His mom was a drunk who had smacked him around, and he'd still come out to her in high school. He got kicked in the nuts so hard that he had to skip two days of school. But he'd still sucked it up and told her.

Hunter was a fucking adult, and he was too scared to tell people he was gay. Jeremiah didn't understand why Quentin would want to be with someone that weak.

Jeremiah walked around the outside of the group of people, nobody really paying him any mind. He did get close once to see two individuals fighting. For a moment, he got so caught up in the excitement that he forgot that he was there to see what Quentin and Hunter were up to.

They'd been vague back at their house when Jeremiah heard them talking before they realized he was there. Part of him wished he had just turned around and left.

He continued around the group, keeping an eye out for Hunter and Quentin when he spotted them near what might be called the front since there was an opening in the crowd.

A skinny wolf-shifter with greasy hair was shaking his head. "I'm not giving you my phone number unless you fight," he said to Hunter.

"I can't fight tonight, but I want to in the future. What happens when I can't get ahold of Trey?" Hunter said. "You know I'm a good fighter. I make you money."

The skinny guy looked to a larger guy next to him, who shrugged.

"How long are you going to be out for?" the skinny male asked.

"I don't know. A month."

"*A month*? No fucking way."

Quentin stepped forward. "I'll fight in his place."

No. Jeremiah didn't want Quentin to get hurt.

He narrowed his eyes. If it wasn't for stupid Hunter, Quentin wouldn't have to fight. He had to wonder if Quentin would have ever fought for him like that.

Probably not.

And that just pissed him off more.

Skinny Guy snorted. "You can't fight worth shit."

Quentin pursed his lips into a thin line. "You've only seen me fight once. Give me another chance."

Skinny Guy just laughed in response.

What an asshole. He didn't have to laugh at Quentin.

"Tell you what," Quentin said. "I'll fight Tank. If I win, you'll let me fight in Hunter's place for the next month."

Hunter put his hand on Quentin's arm and shook his head.

Jeremiah deduced that Tank was the big guy, and he had to agree with the vampire. Quentin was going to get himself killed.

Right as Jeremiah was about to step up and stop Quentin —or at least try—Skinny Guy spoke again, "I'll tell *you* what. If you fight me and win and Hunter finds a replacement for him for the next fight, I'll give you my number and let you continue to fight."

Jeremiah breathed a sigh of relief. Quentin could totally take Skinny Guy.

"So, you want Quentin to fight, but you still want me to find someone else?" Hunter clarified.

"Yes. I want another vampire like you."

"Like me?"

"One who doesn't care if he lives or dies."

Quentin looked at Hunter with sad eyes.

Jeremiah wanted to punch someone. Maybe he needed to get up there and fight.

But first, he needed to make Hunter pay for putting Quentin in this position.

"How about this?" Quentin countered. "If Hunter promises to finds a replacement for himself, you give us both your phone numbers now. We don't want to miss our chance to fight because if we're going to do this, we're going to do this. And I'll fight you tonight and win. You don't have to wait."

Skinny Guy laughed. "Deal."

He rattled off some numbers, and Hunter put them in his phone. When he was done, he stuck his cell in his back pocket, and that was where Jeremiah's idea began to form.

Quentin took off his shirt and prepared to fight, hopping on the balls of his feet.

Jeremiah admired him. He'd thought Quentin was sexy from the first moment he met him, and his attraction to the other man hadn't faded, even with Hunter in the picture.

As Hunter's focus was turned to Quentin and Skinny Guy starting their fight, Jeremiah strode casually behind him. Not so quickly as to draw attention, but fast enough that he wouldn't know who'd just stolen the phone out of his pocket, if he noticed.

Which he didn't, and Jeremiah patted himself on the back.

As a kid, when his mom had been passed out on the couch, Jeremiah had needed to find ways to feed himself. He'd become an expert pickpocket by the age of twelve. He hadn't found it necessary to do in years since he'd grown up, gone to school, and gotten a job that put food on the table.

He was pretty proud that he still had the skills even if he didn't need them.

Jeremiah headed around to the back of the crowd and tried to see the fight, but he couldn't keep watching. Skinny Guy was stronger than he looked.

Jeremiah turned away until the fight was over and figured out what he was going to do next.

FORTY-ONE

RAVEN GENTLY CLOSED the door to her bedroom, and she silently walked away as she breathed a sigh of relief.

It had taken some convincing for Virginia and Calli to stay the night at the house. When Damien had explained to their parents what was going on, they had been all for it. Calli's mom had broken out in tears when Damien told her their daughter most likely had already had sex with men for money. And Virginia's mom was determined for it not to happen to her daughter.

Now, the trick was getting the two girls to talk because, so far, they'd refused to say much.

Raven wanted to walk into the after-school center and haul Monica's ass out of there, but the reality was, it probably wouldn't stop the sex trafficking ring. Damien and Raven needed to find out who was behind it, so they could take it apart from the top down.

And if humans were leading it, then they needed to get the police involved. Shifters were not allowed to punish humans the way they could punish other shifters. And if humans were the ones running the trafficking, then they needed to be arrested and put in prison.

The whole thing was a mess, and Raven hoped that Eldon would shed some light on the subject now that it seemed like he and Kendall were together, but Eldon had been called into work.

Kendall had phoned him, and he was the one who had suggested they keep the girls at the house that night. He would talk to them in the morning. Maybe a police detective could get more information out of them than their alpha could. She hated to think it because it was cliché, but kids today didn't have any respect for their elders.

Raven knocked on Kendall's open door.

Kendall looked up from her computer. "Hey."

"Hey, the two girls are finally asleep, so I'm going to head to bed."

Kendall had offered to stay up that night and keep watch in case the young women tried to sneak out. She was always itching for more responsibility since she'd become pregnant, so she'd volunteered immediately.

Lachlan was posted downstairs, and he had some sort of alarm on both girls' phones that were set to go off if either of them went fifteen feet from the house.

Having both of them keep an eye out reassured Raven that she could get some much-needed rest since she didn't know what the next day would bring. She wasn't supposed to go to the after-school center until the following day, but she was sure she'd have her hands full with Virginia and Calli tomorrow.

"Okay, I'm on it." Kendall tilted her head. "You sure you don't want to sleep here? I can go out into the hall and keep watch."

Raven laughed. "Uh, no. I've heard how much sex you and Eldon have been having in there. You probably need to burn your sheets instead of washing them."

Pink colored Kendall's cheeks. "You try being a horny pregnant woman."

"No, thanks." Raven wasn't ready to be a mom yet. Not that she even had a mate to get her pregnant.

"It'll happen. You just wait."

"We'll see."

"You sure you'll be okay sleeping with Tweedledee and Tweedledum?" Kendall asked, referring to Chase and Ranulf. "You might end up pregnant after all."

"Not if I don't have sex with them during my heat."

"Hmm...I noticed you said, 'during my heat.' You could have just left it as not having sex with them."

Raven rolled her eyes. "I'm not having this conversation."

Kendall shrugged. "Okay. But I'll see you in the morning." She wiggled her eyebrows.

"Get your mind out of the gutter. And, yes, we'll talk in the morning. Just let me know if you hear one of them even get up and do anything more than go to the bathroom."

Kendall mockingly saluted Raven. "Aye, aye, captain."

"Good night, Kendall," she said with a smile as she turned around and left.

"Good night, Raven."

Raven continued down the hall to Chase and Ranulf's room. The guys had been nice to offer to sleep in one bed together, so she could have the other.

But part of her didn't want to sleep in a separate bed. She'd had a long day, and tomorrow wasn't looking good either. She had half a mind to make Chase and Ranulf prove that a threesome could be more exciting than the one she'd had in the past. They'd told her that she just hadn't had a threesome with the right guys. Maybe they were right.

Or maybe they were wrong, and she'd have to lie to them when they asked her how it was.

That thought had her cringing as she walked into their

bedroom. She didn't want to hurt their feelings. Although those two could stand to be taken down a peg or two. They didn't exactly have small egos.

"Ranulf, Chase?" Raven called out when she didn't see them.

"In here," a muffled voice sounded from behind the half-shut bathroom door.

She walked over and pushed the door open further as she said, "Hey, the girls are asleep, and I'm going to…" Raven trailed off, losing her train of thought.

Chase was shirtless and brushing his teeth. In the mirror, her eyes traveled from his treasure trail down to his open jeans where she could see the very top of his dick. Apparently, Chase didn't have on underwear.

She looked in the other direction as Ranulf stepped out of the shower with just a towel hanging loosely in front of him. If it dropped, she would get to see his—

"Raven," Chase said.

She turned as he spit in the sink, his back muscles flexing as he bent over. He stood and used a towel to wipe his mouth.

His brow furrowed in the mirror. "Are you okay? You stopped talking mid-sentence."

He turned around and leaned against the counter, his jeans opening a little bit more. She wanted to push the denim off him and see how big he was.

Ranulf came over to her, his towel now around his waist, and felt her forehead. He had drops of water running down his chest that she wanted to lick off. "She doesn't have a fever."

"Yet she's in some kind of trance," Chase said.

Raven turned and walked out of the bathroom, suddenly hot and unable to breathe. She fanned herself with her shirt, pulling and pushing it back toward her body. But it wasn't enough, and out of nowhere, her clothes were too much.

She yanked her shirt over her head and pushed her pants down at the same time.

As one would expect, that didn't work too well, but Raven couldn't seem to concentrate enough to remove one piece of clothing at a time.

But then Chase and Ranulf were there.

"Hey, hey, let us help you with that," Chase said.

"We got you," Ranulf added as he grabbed on to her shirt for her and pulled it over her head.

Chase drew her pants down off her hips and sat down on his heels to pull the legs off her feet. Raven leaned back against Ranulf's chest and let them take care of her.

Chase raised himself up onto his knees and cursed. He cupped her ass and pushed his face to her crotch as he inhaled. "Fuck, Raven, you smell amazing."

She whimpered.

Ranulf ran his hands down her sides. "Let us take care of you, baby girl."

She pictured both of them taking her. Holding her down as they fucked her.

"Damn," Ranulf said. "You like the sound of that, don't you?"

Raven picked up his hands and put them on her breasts.

"I'll take that as a yes," Chase said.

FORTY-TWO

CHASE GRASPED the waist of her panties and pulled them down her legs as Ranulf took off her bra. Chase lifted one leg, took off her underwear, and then lifted the other. But after her panties were gone, he put her leg on his shoulder and his head between her thighs.

Raven arched her back as Chase ran his tongue over her clit and sucked it into his mouth. She wanted to touch something, too, so she reached behind her and pushed Ranulf's towel off his hips. She blindly grasped for his cock and gasped when she found it.

Ranulf was huge.

He grunted and put his hand on hers to ease her grip. "It's okay. It's not going anywhere," he said right next to her ear.

"But…but I want to…" She moaned as Chase hit a particularly sensitive spot. "Touch you," she quickly finished before she shouted, "Oh fuck," and exploded all over Chase's face.

Now limp, she let go of Ranulf's erection as he picked her up and carried her over to his bed. He laid her down. "How does she taste?" he asked Chase.

He got off the floor and grinned. "Just as good as she did the other night."

"Excellent," Ranulf said and lay down on the bed between her legs.

"Not again," she said in a voice that was more surprise than complaining.

Ranulf opened up her lips and blew on her pussy, making her jump. "Damn, she's sensitive."

"Right?" Chase said as he pushed off his jeans. "She's like a live wire."

She should tell them she was right there, but there was something hot about them talking about her like she wasn't even there.

Ranulf gently pushed two fingers inside her. "So wet and tight, too." He bent his fingers toward her G-spot, and she arched off the bed. "Damn, I can't wait to feel all that heat around me."

"Same." Chase lay down beside her as Ranulf bent his head to her clit and rubbed his fingers inside her.

Chase cupped her breasts and pulled a nipple into his mouth. Wanting to touch something again, she ran her hand down his six-pack until she found his cock.

She should have known he would be huge, too.

She hadn't realized what a turn-on big dicks were until Ranulf had her coming once more. He came up and lay down on the other side of her, taking her other breast in his mouth and sucking on her tight bud.

She'd had two orgasms, and she was still as turned on as ever.

Both Ranulf and Chase lifted their heads and made eye contact.

"I think it's time," Ranulf said.

"Agreed," Chase said.

"It's time for what?" Raven asked.

Ranulf pulled her up on her side and over his body. He placed her legs on either side of his hips and squeezed her ass. He looked her in the eyes. "It's time for Chase and me to fuck you now. You okay with that?"

She swallowed. "At the same time?"

Chase got behind her and grabbed her hips. "Nah, baby. It'll be a while before you're ready to do that. We need to work up to that." He pushed a finger inside her. He added another and then another until she was moaning. Chase wrapped her hair around his wrist and gently pulled her head back. "You ready?"

It's now or never.

She nodded, and Chase pushed inside her as he let her hair go.

"*Ohhhhhhh,*" she cried out, and her head fell to Ranulf's chest.

He cupped her face and pulled her mouth to his. He licked inside her mouth as Chase's cock thrust inside her pussy.

Chase felt incredible, and soon, she was slamming her butt back against his pelvis.

Chase pulled on her hair again, drawing her head back so he could kiss her. When he let go of her hair, he said, "Oh, here she goes again."

He pushed her hair off to the side as he bit down on her shoulder, and another orgasm hit her body, making her legs shake.

Chase slapped her ass and pulled out of her. And within milliseconds, Ranulf grabbed her hips and pulled her down onto his waiting dick.

"*Goddamn it,*" she shouted.

Behind her, Chase pulled her into a sitting position, so she could ride Ranulf. Chase cupped her breasts, and she leaned against him and rotated her hips. The new angle hit a different spot inside her, and she was shocked to find out she might come again.

She'd always been mulitorgasmic, which was one of the reasons she'd had a threesome years ago in the first place. It wasn't fair that only one guy got to get her off. Ironically, she hadn't come even once during that encounter, and she'd decided it was the one and only time she'd do that.

But so far, she'd come three times with a fourth right around the corner. Could she really do it once more?

Ranulf seemed to think so. He jerked his hand to the left, and Chase carefully let her go, so she wouldn't fall over before Ranulf rolled them until he was on top of her. He lifted her leg in the crook of his elbow and began to ride her.

He felt so fucking good, and she instinctively arched her neck.

Chase lay down beside her. "You going to come?"

She nodded her head.

"You want Ranulf to bite you like I did?"

She nodded a second time.

"Tell him." Chase kissed her hard and pulled away. "Tell Ranulf what you want."

She looked at Ranulf. "Bite me and make me come."

Ranulf smiled and went right for her neck. As soon as his teeth hit her, her pussy started contracting as she exploded again.

When her body settled down, Ranulf fell to the other side of her, and she closed her eyes.

But seconds later, they popped open. She lifted her head and looked at both of them and at their hard dicks. "Neither of you came."

Chase pushed himself up on one elbow and smiled, and Ranulf smiled back like there was something only they both knew.

He turned his gaze her way and smirked. "Oh, we're not done with you yet."

She dropped her head to the pillow. "You're going to kill me."

Ranulf picked up her hand and brought it to his lips. "We're going to make you feel more alive than ever."

She had no idea that, by morning, she'd be covered in bite marks on her neck with handprints on her ass and cum between her legs…yet she'd have fallen asleep, satiated beyond belief.

FORTY-THREE

QUENTIN GAVE Hunter a fist bump as they walked to his SUV. "We did it," he said just loud enough to be heard over the cheering behind him.

"Yeah, we did," Hunter agreed as Quentin unlocked his vehicle. Opening their doors, the two of them got in. "We got the phone number, you beat Wayne, *and* you kicked that guy's ass they'd set you up to fight with," Hunter continued once they were inside. He looked Quentin up and down and narrowed his eyes. "Did you purposely lose to me the other night?"

Quentin grinned at Hunter. "Full disclosure?"

"Uh…yeah."

Quentin chuckled to himself. "I did consider going easy on you the other night because I didn't want to fight you. But you fucking brought it, and I had to step up, or you would have left me for dead. So, no, I did not purposely lose. You have a mean streak, Esmund."

Hunter laughed. "I had some pent-up anger to fuel my strength. I sure am relieved you won the fight with Wayne though."

"It wasn't too hard, but he's stronger than he looks." Quentin frowned and sniffed the air.

"What's wrong?"

"This is going to sound weird, but I swear I smelled Jeremiah for a second."

Hunter lifted his nose and inhaled. He looked at Quentin. "I got nothing."

"Hmm. Weird."

Jeremiah had never been in his vehicle.

"Maybe it's from seeing him earlier. Did you shake his hand or hug him good-bye?"

"No, but you're probably right," Quentin agreed for Hunter's sake, but he didn't quite feel like that was the answer.

Hunter didn't need to worry about that though. He had enough on his mind, and he needed to heal. Jeremiah was Quentin's ex, and he'd figure out what the deal was on his own.

Quentin handed his keys to Hunter. "Can you unlock the glove compartment and grab my phone?"

"Sure." Hunter took the keys and made quick work of getting the compartment open. He gave back Quentin his phone and the keys.

Quentin checked his missed calls and text messages. Nothing from Jeremiah, and that made him feel better. Not hate messages or pleading with Quentin to change his mind. Maybe he really had smelled Jeremiah because he had seen him earlier that night.

"Oh shit," Hunter said.

Alarmed, Quentin quickly looked away from his cell. "What's wrong?"

Hunter was patting himself all over. "The phone you gave me, it's gone."

"*Fuck.*"

Hunter's eyes were wide. "I swear I put it in my back pocket, but now, I can't find it." He groaned in frustration. "I should have kept it in my hand. I should have known it would fall out."

Quentin took a deep breath in and exhaled slowly. Now was not the time to panic. "It's going to be okay. This is why we used a burner. No one but the police can trace it back to us. We'll just have to try to get Wayne's and Tank's phone numbers again." He put his hand on the back of Hunter's neck. "It's not the end of the world."

Quentin dropped his arm and leaned back in his seat. He didn't want Hunter to feel bad, but he couldn't help but feel defeated. Wayne and Tank were going to be suspicious when Quentin and Hunter asked for their numbers again.

"Oh, I have the phone numbers."

Quentin whipped his head around. "What? Where?"

Hunter tapped his head. "Right here. Haven't I ever told you that I'm a numbers whiz?"

Quentin laughed in disbelief and pure relief. "No, you haven't."

Hunter smiled smugly. "I am."

He shoved his cell into Hunter's hand. "Hurry up and text those numbers to Eldon before you forget."

Hunter scoffed, insulted, "I'm not going to forget."

Quentin dragged his eyes down Hunter's body, letting the vampire know he was thinking of sex. "Let me rephrase. Text those numbers to Eldon before I *make you* forget."

Hunter leaned over the center console and kissed Quentin. "That's more like it."

Quentin started up his SUV, put it in drive, and slowly maneuvered around the cars parked around them as Hunter sent off a text to Eldon.

With their job done, Quentin wasn't going to worry about the missing phone or Jeremiah the rest of the night. He'd worry about that tomorrow. Tonight, he was going to focus on finding the nearest hotel and being alone with Hunter.

Jeremiah sat in his car in the shadows and waited for everyone to leave now that the fights were over. He planned to confront the Wayne guy and tell him that Hunter was a Guardian. The phone he held in his hand was proof. Jeremiah hadn't been able to get it unlocked, but he'd bet that someone in Wayne's line of work could.

Once Jeremiah exposed Hunter, there was no way they'd let him fight again. And Jeremiah secretly hoped that they would punish Hunter for lying to them. Jeremiah just had to make sure he kept Quentin out of the way when that went down.

When there was no one but Wayne, the big male, and himself, Jeremiah got out of his car. There were two other vehicles left, but Jeremiah didn't want Wayne to leave first. He had hoped to talk to Wayne without the huge guy around, so he snuck around Wayne's car as the shifter was putting stuff in his trunk, away from the huge man's line of sight.

"Hey," Jeremiah said before Wayne could close his trunk.

Wayne twirled around. "Who the fuck are you?"

Jeremiah heard the sound of the big guy's engine starting and the crunch of tires as it drove away. "I'm a friend."

Wayne scoffed, "You're not my fucking friend. Now, what the fuck do you want?"

"I have something for you."

Wayne shook his head, shut his trunk, and walked in the opposite direction. "I'm not interested."

Jeremiah chased after him. "You're going to want to see this." He couldn't believe this Wayne guy wouldn't even hear him out.

Wayne opened his car door and rested his arm on the top. "Look, I'm sure you think you know what I want because you came to a fight." He leaned in close. "But I don't give a fuck what kind of proposition you have for me. You can go find your own way to make money. What I have here is a family business, and we don't bring in outsiders." He dropped his arm and turned away.

Jeremiah gritted his teeth. If this jerk would just give him two minutes, he would like what Jeremiah had to say.

"Hey, asshole, why don't you just listen to me before you make any rash judgments?"

Wayne whirled around, grabbed Jeremiah's shirt in his fist, and slammed him against the car. "You little shit. You don't fucking talk to me like that." He lifted his opposite arm and punched Jeremiah in the face twice.

Jeremiah instinctively tried to push Wayne away, but the guy was too strong. Panic flooded his body, and his fight-or-flight instinct kicked in. Jeremiah shifted his hand and swiped at Wayne with his claws.

In a flash, Wayne went from punching him to taking a step back. Blood dripped down his neck, and he widened his eyes at Jeremiah in shock. He slowly raised a hand and put it to his neck. When he pulled it away, Wayne stared down at his bloody palm. He lifted his gaze to Jeremiah and whispered, "I'm going to kill you for this."

Jeremiah pushed his shoulder into Wayne, like a football tackle, and knocked the guy off his feet. There was a crunch as Wayne's head hit the ground, but Jeremiah didn't care.

He was pissed now. Pissed at Hunter for making Quentin fall in love with him. Pissed at Quentin for being too stupid to see that Hunter was only going to hurt him. Pissed at Wayne for scaring him. And pissed at himself for getting scared. Hunter wouldn't have let Wayne scare him like that. And that was what pissed Jeremiah off the most. It was no wonder that Quentin wanted Hunter and not him.

Jeremiah threw Hunter's phone down on Wayne's chest as

hard as he could. "Hunter's not who you think he is, asshole. That's all I was trying to tell you."

Jeremiah spun on his heel and walked away. He hoped Wayne woke up with a massive headache and a big case of regret. The guy deserved it.

FORTY-FOUR

KENDALL PACED AROUND the living room, waiting for Eldon to finish speaking with Damien.

Eldon had helped Damien take Calli and Virginia to their homes and talked to their parents. Both girls had opened up more this morning, but it turned out, they didn't know much more than what Raven had already overheard. Calli was the only one who had participated in a party. But she had been picked up, taken to an unknown location, and dropped off when she was finished.

Eldon was sure that even if Calli had remembered more, any evidence would be long gone. It was disheartening, to say the least. Now that Kendall was about to be a mom, she couldn't imagine anyone taking advantage of her child like that. It made her sick.

And while it wasn't much comfort, the two girls had been pulled from the after-school program. They would still need a lot of love and therapy to help them through what they'd already gone through, but at least they wouldn't have to endure any more.

Unfortunately, there were many more out there. Calli had

said that she had only recognized one other girl at the party out of about ten. How they were ever going to find them was beyond Kendall. Right now, it seemed like a hopeless task.

Kendall checked the time on her phone. If they were going to make her doctor's appointment, they only had about five minutes before they absolutely had to be driving.

"What's wrong?" Raven asked, coming down the stairs.

"We're going to be late. Maybe I should take off without Eldon."

She had woken up that morning, excited that he was going to see the doctor with her, but he hadn't shown his face for an hour now. Maybe he didn't want to go.

"I don't know, Kendall. He's already missed so much. Don't give him another chance to be resentful of you."

"What do I do?"

"Go knock on the door and tell him it's time to go," Raven suggested as if the answer was obvious.

Kendall looked in the direction of Damien's office and chewed on her lip.

"Ah," Raven said.

Kendall frowned at her friend. "Ah what?"

"You think he's going to want to stay here. You're afraid to go tell him because you don't want to hear him say no."

Kendall changed her expression to cool and nonchalant. "That's not it at all."

Raven's mouth opened in a silent gasp. "That's why you didn't tell him you were pregnant."

"I don't know what you're talking about."

Raven hurried over and threw her arms around Kendall. "Poor Kendall. You're afraid of being rejected."

Kendall pushed Raven away. "Get away. You smell more like sex than a teenage human who jerks off ten times a day."

Raven laughed and shook her finger at Kendall. "Now, you're trying to push me away." She bumped her hip against

Kendall's. "Girl, if you knew the way Eldon watched you when you weren't looking, you wouldn't worry so much."

"Really?" *Don't get excited, Kendall.* "I mean, that's nice."

Raven put her arm around Kendall and rested her head on her shoulder. "Don't worry so much. He likes you, and you like him."

Kendall put her head on top of Raven's. "Thanks." She lifted her head, wrinkled her nose, and playfully elbowed Raven away.

"Do I smell that bad?" Raven asked. "I took a long shower."

"You don't smell that bad or like sex. You do smell like Ranulf and Chase."

"So, you're saying everyone's going to know?"

Kendall laughed. "They already know. You, my friend, are not a quiet lover."

Raven turned red, and Kendall pulled the collar of her shirt back.

"Plus, you are covered in marks. Do we have a mating to celebrate?"

Raven shook Kendall off. "No. Those are sex marks." She pulled her shirt up to her ears. "You just leave me alone."

"I'll leave you alone when you leave me alone."

Raven narrowed her eyes. "You're evil. But it's good practice for when you're a mom."

A door opened, and Eldon called out, "I'm coming. Don't leave without me."

Raven smiled. "I told you."

"Told her what?" Eldon asked as he walked into the room.

"Nothing," Kendall said quickly. "Just girl stuff. You okay to go? If you need to stay and work with Damien, I can go alone."

Eldon picked up her hand. "Oh no, your days of going

213

alone are over." He took off for the door, tugging Kendall with him.

She glanced behind her to see Raven grinning from ear to ear.

It's going to be okay, she mouthed.

She squeezed Eldon's hand and hoped her friend was right because there was one more thing that she hadn't told him. She just hoped he wouldn't hate her for it when it came out.

FORTY-FIVE

ELDON'S HEART was so full right now that he didn't know if he could take any more excitement.

The doctor had let Eldon listen to his baby's heartbeat, and then because she was the coolest doctor ever, she pulled out a handheld ultrasound machine and showed him what the baby looked like.

He had known Kendall was pregnant, and he had felt the baby kick, but there was something about seeing him in black and white on the screen that made it that much more real.

Eldon kissed Kendall on the head as the doctor toweled off her belly. "That was amazing. Thank you," he said to the doctor.

She smiled. "No problem. Kendall has been talking about you since the beginning. I hear you're a famous detective. I'm so glad you could finally make it in."

"Me, too," Eldon said as he watched out of the corner of his eye while Kendall hid her face. He might not have known her long, but he knew she was embarrassed.

She hopped down from the table and straightened her clothes.

"I'll see you in two weeks," the doctor said and exited the room.

"You talked about me, huh?" Eldon asked.

Kendall sighed. "It's not a big deal. You're the father." She stalked out of the room, not even waiting to see if he followed.

Eldon picked up his speed to catch up with her. For a pregnant woman, she could move pretty fast.

"Kendall."

She kept going.

"Hey. Kendall."

She sighed again and turned around.

Irritation was written all over her face, but he wasn't going to let that ruin his great mood. Plus, he could tell something was bothering her.

"What do you want, Eldon?"

He picked up her hand and walked them to his car at a much slower pace than Kendall had been going. "I was thinking about the name Conrad."

"I thought you'd like it since it's your last name." She looked so sad; it almost broke Eldon's heart.

"I do. I think it's an excellent name," he said to make her feel better.

"But…"

"But Conrad Conrad sounds kind of silly, don't you think? I mean, unless our kid is going to be famous, but the chances of that happening are slim to none."

She pulled her hand from his. "Who said the baby is going to have your last name?"

Eldon pretended to be confused. "I guess…I just thought… don't you want him to have the same last name as you?"

Her brow furrowed. "But my last name is Walker."

"Now, but not once we are mated. Unless you want to keep your last name. You could always hyphenate. I know it's the twenty-first century, but if I change my last name, I will never hear the end of it at work. What can I say? Men suck. So, on that note, Conrad Walker-Conrad sounds even worse than just Conrad—"

Kendall stepped in front of Conrad and slapped her hand over his mouth. "I have never heard you talk so much in my life."

"Sorry," he said, but it came out sounding like, *Sowwy*.

She slowly drew her hand away. "Don't be sorry. I'm just… I don't understand."

Eldon pulled her into his arms. "Don't understand what?"

He leaned down and rubbed his nose against her neck. He pushed her shirt to the side, so he could suck on her skin. All she had to do was say the word, and he'd mark her right now.

He heard her swallow next to his ear.

"You really want to be my mate?" she asked hesitantly.

"Without a doubt," he said, not lifting his head. "Say yes," he whispered and nipped at her.

Kendall stepped away. "I need to tell you something first."

Eldon frowned. "Okay. What is it?"

"I did some research, and I'm the reason I got pregnant."

Eldon smiled. "I don't know what you learned in biology class, but I was taught that it takes two."

She grabbed on to the front of his shirt. "I'm serious, Eldon. Remember after we were rescued and we slept together again in my room?"

"Babe, that's been imprinted in my mind since that night."

"Then, you remember how I lifted myself off you after you came and sank back down, and we both came again?"

Eldon looked around as he adjusted his now-hard dick. "Jesus, you can't talk like that when we're out in public."

Kendall shook him. "Eldon, you're not paying attention. I'm pretty sure that's when I got pregnant. That's why you have the barbs. I pulled you out, triggering my ovulation. It had only been a few hours since my heat ended. Or at least, that's what I thought. But now, I think it was just on the declining end. I'm the reason you're going to be a father. And I did it without your consent."

Eldon felt horrible. She looked miserable, all while he was getting more turned on. Listening to her talk about how he'd gotten her pregnant was making him so hard that he wasn't sure if he could drive without some relief.

He cupped her cheeks in his hands. "Did you get pregnant on purpose? No. Were you trying to trick me? No."

"How can you be so sure?"

"Because I know you. And you know what else I remember from that night?"

"No."

"I asked you what made you pull me out and push me back in like you did. Do you remember what you said?"

She shook her head.

"You told me, 'I don't know. I just did.' Which tells me that your wolf was in charge. And your wolf knew that it wanted to have my baby." He unclenched her hands from his shirt and hauled her into his arms. "And I came again, which I think means my cat wanted you to have my baby. Our animal halves already decided we're supposed to be together. And I don't know about you, but I'm not going to argue with them."

Kendall sniffled.

Eldon pulled her away. "Are you okay?"

She nodded.

"Then, why are you crying?"

"I'm just really, really happy."

Eldon laughed and embraced her once more. "Will you let me mark you now?"

"Here?" she said against his chest, her voice sounding shocked.

"Yes. I don't want to wait to get home."

She gasped and looked up at him. "Home? Where are we going to live?"

"We'll figure out the semantics later." He growled, "Now, give me your neck."

"We can't have sex in a parking lot."

He yanked her off her feet and shoved his face into her neck. "I know. We'll do that when we get home. But first, I'm going to make you mine." Eldon yanked her shirt out of the way and sank his teeth into her shoulder.

Kendall whimpered and shook in his arms.

Eldon froze and slowly withdrew his teeth. He raised his head and looked down at her. "Did you just come?"

"No," she said, her cheeks turning bright pink.

Eldon laughed. "Fucking liar. I told you, your wolf wants me." He kissed her. "I can't wait to get you home." He set her on her feet just as his phone rang.

He pulled it out of his pocket and looked at the screen before he groaned. "It's work." He swiped the green button to answer. "Conrad."

"I need you at crime scene," said Briscoe, a fellow detective he worked with.

Eldon swore under his breath. "It's my day off."

"I know, but you're going to want to see this."

"Okay. I just have to drop my fiancée off, and then I'll be there." It was the closest human thing Kendall was to him right now.

"Fiancée?"

Eldon grinned. "I'll tell you about it later."

"Congratulations."

"Does this mean I don't need to come in?"

"You wish. Get your ass over here, Conrad. I'll text you the address."

FORTY-SIX

ELDON STARED down at the body of one Wayne Dahl and sighed. "Fuck my life."

"What was that?" the crime scene photographer asked, pulling his camera away from his face.

"Nothing."

The guy shrugged and went back to taking photographs.

Briscoe came up behind him. "The lab just confirmed the serial number on the phone. It's the one assigned to Officer Rawling."

Eldon didn't say anything because he'd already known it would be. The dead wolf-shifter reeked of Quentin, and the phone in Wayne Dahl's pocket matched the phone number Quentin had sent Eldon last night.

"What did he use on his neck?" Detective Briscoe asked, squatting near Wayne's neck.

Eldon knew what had been used—wolf claws—but he couldn't tell anyone else that. "I don't know. We'll have to wait for the medical examination to come back."

Briscoe stood and looked at Eldon. "What in the hell went

FORTY-SIX

ELDON STARED down at the body of one Wayne Dahl and sighed. "Fuck my life."

wrong last night? You said this was supposed to be an easy assignment."

"That's what I'd like to know." Also, why the hell had Quentin neglected to tell him that he'd killed someone?

(

The best part of getting a hotel room was that Quentin and Hunter had gotten to stay in bed with each other all day. They'd ordered room service and not left at all until they checked out after dark.

It was going to suck, going back home and pretending to be only friends, but if the two of them got to do this once or twice a month, Quentin could live with being a secret boyfriend.

When they reached the end of the driveway, Quentin pulled his vehicle off to the side.

"What are you doing?"

"I want to give you one last kiss before we have to go into the house."

Hunter smiled. "I like the sound of that."

Quentin put his hand on the back of Hunter's neck and kissed him long and deep. When he broke the kiss, they were both breathing hard. "Just so you know, I'm going to have a hard time, not sneaking into your room tonight."

"Who says you can't?"

Quentin grinned as he put his SUV in drive and pulled into the long driveway.

The two walked into the house, all smiles, but when they made it into the living room, they stopped short.

Everyone in the house was sitting around, and they all looked grim. Damien and Eldon were standing with their arms crossed, and there was a heaviness in the air that could only be explained as foreboding.

Damien met Quentin's eyes. "Why don't you have a seat." It was a statement, not a question.

Hunter and Quentin sat on the couch, and Quentin had to resist grabbing Hunter's hand.

"What's going on?" Quentin asked.

"Where were you last night?" Damien asked him.

Hunter turned pale beside him. Quentin wanted to tell him it'd be okay. He wasn't going to out Hunter.

"Hunter and I went to the fight for a couple of hours, and then we stopped and got a hotel room, so we wouldn't have to drive home."

"Whose idea was it?"

Quentin didn't understand what this interrogation was about. If it was because he and Hunter had slept together, they were not the shifters he'd thought they were.

"It was mine," Quentin said. "Hunter was tired, and he'd had a big night."

Damien turned to Hunter. "Is this true?"

Hunter nodded. "Yes."

"So, you went to the fight together and went to the hotel together?"

"Yes," Quentin answered Damien's question.

"And did you get separate rooms?"

Quentin considered telling the truth because he didn't like lying, but fuck them for even asking these questions in the first place.

"Yes, not that it's any of your business."

Damien pinched the bridge of his nose and closed his eyes while Eldon cursed.

Hunter looked at Quentin in confusion, but he had no idea what was going on either.

Damien dropped his arm and straightened his back. "So, if you slept in separate rooms, there's no one to confirm that you didn't leave again last night."

Quentin bit his lip. This wasn't good. He'd been a cop long enough to know when someone was fishing for an alibi. All Quentin had to do was tell them the name of the hotel, and he was sure that the security cameras would show that he hadn't left until they'd checked out, but it would also show him and Hunter kissing right outside the door.

Quentin dropped his head in his hand in defeat. "No. There's no way."

Hunter made a noise beside him, but Quentin quickly pushed his leg into the vampire's, telling him to be quiet.

Quentin looked up. "So, now that we've established that I have no alibi, can you tell me what this is about?"

Eldon stepped forward. "Wayne was found dead today."

Quentin jumped to his feet. "Whoa, whoa, I didn't fucking kill anyone."

"He smelled like you," Damien said.

"That's because I had to fight him." He gestured to Hunter. "Ask Hunter."

"It's true. He wouldn't give us the phone numbers unless Quentin agreed to fight."

"His neck was also cut open with claw marks," Damien added.

Eldon sighed and rubbed his forehead. "There's more than that. Quentin, they found your burner cell right next to the body. All the information is already in the police database. Even if Damien believes you and his word is law, the police know. I've asked for twenty-four hours, but I'm going to have to bring you in."

Quentin looked around the room at his fellow sentinels. They looked sad for him, and to be honest, he was sad for himself, too.

This was why he didn't like keeping a relationship secret.

He glanced back at Hunter.

Fuck it. Hunter was worth it. And if Quentin had to go to jail for the rest of his life, he'd do it.

Quentin stepped toward Eldon with his wrists out. "I understand you need to do what you need to do. I'm a cop, too." Or he *had been* a cop. "I'm ready. You can take me in."

FORTY-SEVEN

WHAT THE FUCK *is Quentin doing?*

Panic and fear taking over, Hunter jumped up from the couch. "You can't take him."

Quentin looked over his shoulder. "Hunter, it's okay. I'll be fine."

"No, it won't be fine." He looked around the room at everyone he'd lived with for the past year until his eyes settled on Eldon. He seemed like the safest one to come out to. "Quentin lied. We shared a room last night."

"That seems like a stupid thing to lie about," Damien said.

"And it doesn't exactly give Quentin an alibi," Eldon added. "Did you fall asleep? How do you know Quentin didn't leave while you were out?" He shook his head sadly. "I'm sorry, but I have to bring him in."

Hunter held up his hand. "Stop." His heart was racing so much that he was afraid he might pass out.

Quentin must have felt it because he put his own hand to Hunter's chest. "You don't have to. It's okay," he said to Hunter.

"No, it's not." All eyes were on him, and he felt as if the

walls were closing in, but he took a few deep breaths. If he could be a Guardian, he could tell everyone he was gay. "Quentin didn't sneak out."

Quentin closed his eyes.

"And I know he didn't sneak out because not only did we share a room, but we also shared a bed."

"*I knew it*," Chase exclaimed.

Quentin opened his eyes and shot Chase a dirty look.

"What time did Wayne die?" Hunter continued because he wasn't done. "Because Quentin and I didn't go to sleep until after eight in the morning."

The room was silent as if no one, besides Chase, knew what to say.

Finally, Damien made a loud noise in celebration and shouted, "Holy hell, I'm so relieved."

Everybody else started clapping, and Quentin stalked over to Hunter and kissed him.

In front of everyone.

When Quentin took a step back, Hunter was sure his face was the color of a tomato.

"You didn't have to tell them," Quentin said.

"Yes, I did. I couldn't let you go to jail for something you didn't do."

Quentin grinned. "If I didn't think I loved you before, now, I know I do."

Hunter's mouth fell open. "You love me?"

"Of course, you idiot. I was going to go to prison to keep your secret."

Hunter wrapped his arms around Quentin. "I love you, too. I think I always have."

The small crowd around them was still clapping for them until Eldon cleared his throat.

Quentin stepped out of Hunter's arms and stood next to him.

"I hate to be the one who shits on this—"

"Cambridge Hotel," Quentin said. "You'll be able to see us on the security cameras. Going in and out of the same room."

Eldon grinned. "Thank you. That's exactly what I needed to hear." He pulled his phone from his pocket and stepped out of the room.

Kendall walked up to them and threw her arms around their shoulders. "I'm so happy for you guys."

Her belly hit Hunter's arm, and he felt something kick him.

Kendall stepped back and put a hand on her stomach. "Sorry. That's Jamison's way of saying he's happy, too."

"Jamison, huh?" Quentin asked.

"Yeah." Kendall grinned shyly. "Eldon and I decided on it today."

"After he marked you as his mate?"

Kendall touched her neck. "Yeah."

Quentin hugged her again. "I'm happy for you, too. You picked a good man."

"Thanks, Quentin."

The other shifters came up and expressed their congratulations.

Hunter had never been so happy to live with this group of individuals as he was now.

Damien was last, and he pulled his mate along with him. "Payton and I are very excited for you both."

"So excited," Payton said.

Damien slapped Hunter on the arm. "You saved the day."

Hunter chuckled. "I don't know about that. And after everyone else finds out…"

Payton put her hand on Hunter's. "I understand a little about vampires and their way of thinking, thanks to Naya. I can't imagine the Guardians exiling you. But if they do, you're welcome here for as long as you want." Her face brightened. "Maybe you can even be the first vampire sentinel."

Damien put his arm around Payton and laughed uncomfortably. "Baby girl, let's not get ahead of ourselves. We can't just make Hunter a sentinel." He met Hunter's eyes, the expression now serious. "But my mate is right about you staying here. We would never kick you out, Hunter. You're welcome to live here as long as you'd like. Especially if you're mated with this guy," he said, pointing to Quentin.

Hunter thought he might actually cry. "Thank you both. I'm going to talk to Dante tomorrow night. Do you think we can keep this between us until then?"

"No problem," Damien said.

As the excitement wore down and everyone either went to work or to their own rooms, Quentin grabbed Hunter's hand and led him upstairs. "Whose room?"

"Yours."

"You sure?"

"Yes. It's where we first made love."

Quentin smiled and pushed his door open. "Welcome to our room, Hunter Rawling," he joked.

Hunter grinned. "Thank you, Quentin Esmund."

The two of them laughed as they closed the door behind them and kissed.

"We'll worry about who takes whose name later," Quentin said.

FORTY-EIGHT

QUENTIN PULLED his shirt over his head before bending down to kiss a sleeping Hunter on the cheek.

The vampire was asleep on his stomach with the sheet around his waist, and Quentin really wanted to hop back into bed.

But there was something he needed to do today.

Hunter stirred and lifted his head off the pillow. "Where are you going?"

"I have a thing I have to take care of." He kissed Hunter on the lips this time. "But I'll be back before dark, so I can go talk to Dante with you."

"Okay." Hunter dropped his face back into his pillow. "Be careful."

"I will."

Quentin quietly left the room, padded down the hall to Kendall's room, and knocked.

There were a few noises behind the door, and less than thirty seconds later, a half-naked Eldon opened it.

Quentin smiled. "Hey, I'm sorry to interrupt, but I think I have a lead on what happened to Wayne. You in?"

"Yes." He turned, ran to the bed, and dropped a kiss on Kendall's lips. "I'll be back." He grabbed the nearest shirt off the floor and two mismatched socks. "Okay, let's go."

"You might want to grab your handcuffs," Quentin told him.

☾

When they pulled up to their destination, Eldon asked, "Where are we?"

"At my ex's house."

"Your ex-boyfriend?" Eldon looked surprised.

"Yeah. Kind of. It was never official, but we dated." Quentin opened his door and reluctantly got out. He didn't want to do this, but it had to be done.

"What are we doing here?" Eldon asked as he exited the vehicle.

"The night of the last fight, I thought I smelled Jeremiah—my ex—in my SUV. He's never been inside it," Quentin pointed out before Eldon could ask. "I thought it was odd but dismissed it because I had just seen him a few hours earlier. But this morning, when I was lying in bed, I remembered what I had smelled."

"And how would that tie him to Wayne?"

"I don't know, but I thought it was worth checking out."

"Since my only lead has a solid alibi, let's do this."

Quentin and Eldon walked up to Jeremiah's door, and Quentin rang the bell.

Jeremiah answered a few minutes later. "Hey, Mom. I didn't—" He swallowed nervously. "Quentin. I wasn't expecting you."

"Do you mind if we come in?"

Jeremiah stepped back. "Uh, no."

They entered the house as Quentin said, "Jeremiah, this is

Eldon. Eldon, this is Jeremiah." He looked right at his ex. "Eldon is a detective with the Minneapolis Police Department."

"Oh. And to what do I owe the honor?" Jeremiah chuckled nervously.

Quentin took his cop stance. Feet spread apart, arms folded, and a no-nonsense look on his face. "You can start by telling me why my vehicle smelled like you the other night after you came to visit me. You've never been in it."

Quentin watched the panic come over Jeremiah's face. He looked like a deer caught in headlights. Quentin might not be a detective, but he knew when a suspect was going to crumble and when he wasn't.

"You can also tell me why you followed me after you left my house."

Quentin had only suspected this, but as the blood drained from Jeremiah's face, he had his answer.

"Son, why don't you tell us what happened that night? We know you didn't mean to kill Wayne."

Quentin raised his eyebrows at Eldon. It looked like Quentin was the bad cop, and Eldon was the good one. He hadn't even known they were playing roles.

Jeremiah swayed and took a step back. "Wayne's dead?"

And there was the proof that Jeremiah had been there.

"How do you know who Wayne is?"

Jeremiah swayed again, and Eldon went over to him and took his arm.

"Why don't you sit down?" He helped Jeremiah into a chair. "Now, tell us what happened."

Jeremiah opened his mouth and spilled the whole story about how he had followed Quentin and Hunter. How he'd stolen the phone from Hunter's pocket because he thought it would get Hunter in trouble. He'd also searched Quentin's vehicle for anything else to take to Wayne but not found anything, and that explained why Quentin had smelled him.

While Jeremiah described what had happened, Quentin had to stand farther and farther away from Jeremiah. He couldn't believe that someone he'd trusted would do something to hurt someone he loved. He'd thought Jeremiah was a better shifter than that.

After Jeremiah told them about how he'd gotten into a fight with Wayne and hadn't meant to kill him, Eldon had him stand up. "I'm sorry, Jeremiah, but I'm going to have to arrest you."

"For what?" Jeremiah asked.

"Manslaughter at least. But it'll be up to the DA and what she wants to charge you with."

"Doesn't Damien decide what happens to me?"

"The body is already in the morgue, and the murder is in the police files. It's beyond shifter control at this point. Now, turn around." Eldon put his cuffs on Jeremiah. "You have the right to remain silent…"

Jeremiah started crying, but Quentin didn't feel bad for him. Jeremiah might get off on self-defense, but he had hurt someone and left him alone to die. Even if the person was bad, it didn't give Jeremiah the right to take things into his own hands.

"I'll call dispatch," Quentin told Eldon and went outside to wait.

Quentin was happy that he wouldn't be charged with Wayne's murder and that they had a confession. He just hated that it was from Jeremiah.

FORTY-NINE

MONICA DAHL SAT in her office at the after-school center and watched the surveillance video one more time. She'd made a good decision when she splurged for small ones that were hidden in the walls. You couldn't put a price on that kind of insurance.

She watched Raven hustle Calli and Virginia outside and into the parking lot before they went out of sight of any cameras. She saw Raven walked back into the center alone, briefly speak with another volunteer, and then turning around a leaving again.

Monica reversed the recording and watched it again.

She'd done this multiple times, but she still couldn't figure out what Raven had been up to. Monica couldn't make out what Raven had said to the girls, and before that, she hadn't been within camera range.

The only places that didn't have cameras were the restrooms and Monica's office.

And Monica would bet money on Raven not being in the restroom, which meant she'd been standing outside Monica's office.

"Damn it," she said, slamming the lid of her laptop closed.

She hadn't felt right about Raven since the night Raven's supposed boyfriend and his friend asked her to the club.

Chase had acted like he was into her, but Monica could tell he wasn't attracted to her. Even a human could tell when someone wasn't interested, and she had the added bonus of being able to smell his lack of attraction to her. He'd been more into Raven than her.

This had all been proven when she slipped a date-rape drug into their shots and watched them from afar. If it hadn't been for some drunken dancers, they probably would have had sex right there on the dance floor.

What Monica hadn't been able to figure out was why Raven and her two friends had invited her. Raven hadn't slipped up since then. Until the other day—when she'd hauled ass out of there with the two girls.

But the girls hadn't come back. Raven was up to no good.

Buzz.

Her phone vibrated on her desk. It was her brother Frank.

"Francis," she answered. "Did you find Wayne?"

Silence.

Monica stood. "Frank, where the hell is Wayne?"

Frank hadn't heard from their brother Wayne since he left the fight they ran last night.

"He's dead."

Monica laughed. "Very funny. Where is he really? Sleeping off a binge? At some bimbo's house?"

There were times she really regretted getting into business with her family. But they were loyal. Her brothers might be idiots occasionally, but they would never betray her.

"I'm not joking, Monica. Someone just came to our apartment. Wayne's dead."

"No. NO!" She took a calming breath. "We're going to find who did this, and we're going to kill him."

"He's already in custody."

That was a shocker. Her brother had been a lowlife criminal his whole life. She was surprised the police had given a damn.

"He is?"

"Yeah. Some guy got into a fight with him, and when Wayne scared him, he attacked."

"Shifter?"

"Yes. Wolf."

"Where did they find Wayne?" She pictured the outside of a bar or a liquor store.

"At the site of the fight. He never left."

She pulled the receiver away from her mouth. "Fuck."

If her brother wasn't already dead, she'd kill him herself. He'd always had a stupid temper.

She moved the mouthpiece back. "Did the police ask you any questions?"

"They just wanted to know what he was doing out there. I told them I didn't know, and they dropped it. I'm guessing they'll be coming to talk to you next."

"Thanks for the heads-up," she said and hung up.

She didn't know if it was a good sign that they'd questioned Frank and not pressed for more answers or if that meant that they'd already known the answers and just wanted to see what Frank would say.

She did not need this on top of the Raven situation.

Sometimes, being in charge wasn't worth the headache.

She went to the front door when the police showed up.

"Hello, ma'am. We'd like to speak to you about your brother," one of the detectives said.

"Yes. Come in."

Raven would have to wait. Today, Monica was going to have to deal with the death of her brother.

FIFTY

HUNTER LED Quentin into the large home where the Guardians lived.

Quentin looked around in amazement as they walked down the hall. "I knew you used to live in a house larger than ours, but I had no idea it was a mansion."

Hunter shrugged. "It's not that big of a deal."

Quentin looked at Hunter like he was crazy. "Says you."

"Let's go," Hunter said, ignoring Quentin's last comment.

Yes, the vampires had money, but it didn't make them any happier. He'd rather be broke with Quentin than rich and alone.

He'd only been halfway out of the closet for one night, but he had never felt so free. And now that he had one foot out, he wanted to be out all the way. Even if it meant losing the people he cared about.

Because he had Quentin.

"Why are you looking at me like that?" Quentin asked.

Hunter smiled. "I'll tell you later." He stopped in front of a door. "We're here."

Quentin squared his shoulders and knocked.

"Come in," Dante said from the other side.

"Do you want me to come in with you?" Quentin asked.

Hunter had originally planned to speak with Dante alone, but now, in the moment, he changed his mind. Quentin was the reason Hunter was where he was in life. Quentin should be there.

"I want you to come in with me. Is that okay?"

Quentin squeezed his shoulder. "You know it is."

"Showtime," Hunter said as he opened the door.

"Hey, Hunter," Dante said with a smile. He turned his eyes to Quentin and frowned. "Quentin."

Hunter looked at Quentin. *What's that about?*

Quentin shrugged, but Hunter knew there was something he wasn't being told. However, it wasn't important now.

"I came to speak to you," Hunter told Dante.

"I gathered that much when you told me you were coming over."

Hunter laughed. *Right.* He hated feeling nervous, but no amount of training had prepared him to tell Dante his sexual orientation.

"Have a seat, Hunter. You, too, Rawling."

They both sat, and Hunter realized that everything he had worked for might come crashing down.

He glanced at Quentin, who mouthed, *It'll be okay.*

Quentin was right. And if Quentin could go to prison for him, then Hunter could lose his job for Quentin.

"Hunter," Dante said and raised his eyebrows.

"Sorry." He shifted to the edge of his chair and tried to look his leader in the eyes, but he couldn't quite do it. He couldn't bear to watch the respect slowly drain from Dante's eyes, so he stared down at his hands. "I've come to let you know that I might have to resign from my position."

"What is this about, Hunter?" Dante said, calmer than Hunter had thought he would be. "I just replaced Lexine after she broke the rules. I can't lose you, too."

Hunter looked up. "Sir, it might not be my choice."

Dante frowned and sat back in his chair. "Hunter, I don't think you've ever called me sir. Please don't start now."

"Sorry."

"Now, spit it out."

Hunter opened his mouth, but no sound came out.

Dante's eyes darted to Quentin and back to Hunter. "Does this have something to do with Quentin?"

"Dante—" Quentin started, but Dante lifted his hand.

"I want to hear it from Hunter."

"Yes, it does," Hunter admitted.

"So, what is it?"

It's now or never. Hunter met Dante's gaze, finding his courage after all. "I'm in love with Quentin." He picked up Quentin's hand and laced their fingers together. "I'm gay."

An immediate calm settled over Hunter.

That wasn't so bad.

"I'm gay," he said again. "And I no longer want to keep it a secret." He took a relaxing breath. No matter what happened now, he knew he'd be okay.

Dante leaned forward and studied Hunter. Then, out of nowhere, a grin split across his face. "It's about fucking time."

Hunter was dumbstruck and sat there in shock while Quentin burst out laughing.

"I…I…I don't understand."

"Hunter, I've known you were gay for a long time."

"Oh my God, does everyone know?"

Dante thought about this. "I don't think so." He smiled. "But that's why I'm the leader, and they're not."

"What—when—how—how did you know?" Hunter asked.

"You've never been interested in a woman, for one. And I

remember the night you went out with Quentin for the first time. That was the most nervous I've ever seen you. And then when Quentin threatened to rip my throat out if I fed you while you were in the hospital, I knew the two of you had to be involved."

Hunter looked at Quentin.

Quentin shrugged. "Guilty," he said with no shame. "I was worried about you." He looked at Dante. "I apologize. It was uncalled for."

"We're good, Rawling. I would do the same if anyone tried to feed Phoenix. But that doesn't mean you didn't owe me that apology."

"Right," Quentin said.

"So, why are you going to quit?" Dante asked Hunter. "And why were you so worried to tell me? I'm mated to a cat-shifter."

"The king and queen," Hunter explained. "I know how they feel about anyone who isn't heteronormative."

"Technically, they are in charge, but I'm the one who runs this show, Hunter. I would never let who you love affect your position here."

Hunter breathed a sigh of relief. "Thank you."

Dante shook his head. "No. Thank you for trusting me enough to tell me." He stood. "How do you feel about telling everyone else? I really think they'd be happy for you."

Quentin squeezed his hand.

"Let's do it."

Dante walked around his desk and opened the door to his office. "Phoenix," he yelled.

The sound of someone falling down the stairs could be heard from where they stood.

"What the hell?" Quentin said, and he and Hunter stood to follow Dante out of the office.

"That's just Ash. He goes down the stairs on his stomach. It always sounds like someone's tripped. It about gave Phoenix and me heart attacks every time we heard it when he first started. Now, we're used to it."

The slapping of little feet pounding on the ground came next until a flying ball of a kid jumped up and landed in Dante's arms. "Dada."

"Hey, little man. Where's Mommy?"

Ash pointed behind him.

"I'm coming. I'm coming," she said as she held on to her belly. It wasn't very big, but it was apparent she was pregnant.

"Congratulations, Dante," Hunter said.

"Thanks. We're pretty excited to give Ash a brother or sister."

"What's up?" Phoenix said when she reached them. "Hey, Quentin. Hey, Hunter."

Dante put his arm around Phoenix. "Hunter and Quentin have some news, and I thought you should be the first to know after me." He nuzzled her cheek. "Since you're my mate and all."

Ash put his hand between his parents and pushed them apart. "No."

"Ash has a jealous streak," she told Hunter and Quentin. "Kind of like his father."

Dante smirked.

"He's not going to be happy when this baby is born and he has to share me."

They all chuckled, and Ash clapped his hands and grinned.

The poor kid had no idea that they were laughing about him.

"So, what did you want to tell me?" Phoenix asked.

Hunter smiled and said the words again, "I'm gay."

Phoenix grinned. "Congratulations."

After Dante and Phoenix, telling everyone else that he was

in a relationship with Quentin was easy. And the hugs and congratulations he received was more than he could have ever expected.

EPILOGUE

LATER THAT NIGHT, Quentin and Hunter lay in bed, holding each other.

"I have a present for you," Quentin said.

Hunter smiled. "Oh, yeah? What's that?"

Quentin sat up and wrapped his arms around his knees. "I know you still have to tell your parents, and there's my family, too. My sister will be back soon."

Hunter sat up. "Yes." He wasn't sure where Quentin was going with this. Quentin's family already knew he was gay. "Are you worried that you have to tell them I'm a vampire?"

"No. Not at all. My parents are a black and white couple who fell in love in the fifties. They're not going to care that you're a vampire."

"Then, what is it?"

"I'm not sure how things are going to be. My sister is doing really well, but she could relapse. And what if she—"

Hunter put his hand on the back of Quentin's neck. "Then, we'll deal with it. Together. And if you have to go to Switzerland or China or...Timbuktu, we'll go together. I love you. And while I haven't met her yet, your sister is my sister. I've never had a sibling, and I'm excited."

Quentin leaned over and brushed his lips against Hunter's. "God, I love you."

"Just don't forget it," he said against Quentin's lips. "Now, what's my present?"

Quentin pulled away and laughed. "Impatient, aren't we?"

"Hey, I reassured you. I comforted you. I told you I love you. Now, gimme."

"Now, you're just going to be let down."

"Tell me, you fool. I'll be the judge of that."

Quentin held out his arms. "It's me."

Hunter tapped his finger to his lips. "Not that I don't appreciate it, but don't I already have you?"

Quentin turned his face away and actually blushed. Hunter could sense the blood rising to Quentin's face.

Quentin looked at Hunter out of the corner of his eye. "I want you to have sex with me."

Hunter frowned. "We've had sex numerous times."

"Technically, I have sex with you." He leaned over, pulled out some lube from the drawer next to him, and put it in Hunter's hands. "I want you to have sex with me."

Hunter's eyes rounded. "Are you sure? I'm okay with not switching roles."

Quentin put his finger to Hunter's lips. "I'm sure." He smiled and withdrew his hand. "And if I'm being honest, I've had the idea in my head since you slipped a finger in my back door at the clinic. I can't stop thinking of you taking me."

If Hunter hadn't been on medication, he doubted he would have been so bold with Quentin that night. He never thought something good would have come out of his head injury. Hunter leaned toward Quentin and kissed him. "This is the best gift I've ever received."

"Really?"

"Really. Now, take off your clothes and get on your back."

Both of them stripped, and Quentin lay on his back in the center of the bed. He helped Hunter prepare his own hole, so he could take him, and Hunter felt like he was going to burst; his dick was so excited.

Hunter sat on his heels by Quentin's ass and rubbed his hard length against Quentin's now-ready opening. "Are you sure about this?" Hunter asked.

Quentin nodded. "Don't be disappointed if I can't get off."

"I won't be. I'll just have to take you in my mouth." He leaned over Quentin and kissed him. "I don't get off every time you're inside me. I promise not to take it personally."

"Okay."

Hunter reached down, grabbed his cock, and slowly pushed into Quentin. "Oh my God, you feel so fucking good."

Hunter had been inside a few women in the past when he tried out hetero sex, but it was nothing—*nothing*—compared to being inside Quentin.

"I'm not going to last long."

Quentin clutched at his back. "That's okay. You can suck me off that much sooner."

Hunter barked out a laugh and began to slowly thrust his hips, not wanting to hurt Quentin.

But soon, Quentin was rocking his pelvis over Hunter's and making the sexiest noises.

Knowing that Quentin was now fully prepared, Hunter didn't hold back and slammed inside Quentin over and over.

"I'm going to come soon," Hunter said next to Quentin's ear.

"Yes. Please. Yes," Quentin said, digging his fingers into Hunter's skin as Hunter drove in and out of him.

"Bite me, Quentin. Mark me. Make me yours."

Quentin rolled Hunter on his back, flipping both of them over, and began to ride him.

Just when Hunter didn't think he could take any more, Quentin pushed his face between Hunter's shoulder and ear and bit down on his neck.

Hunter's climax burst out of him like a bullet from a gun, and he grabbed on to Quentin, never wanting to let go. Quentin grunted and gripped him tightly, and Hunter hoped he was able to enjoy the moment, too.

Slowly, Hunter realized that Quentin was still gently rocking his hips on Hunter's cock and placing kisses on the bite mark on his neck.

Hunter used the last of his strength to say, "That was the best present ever."

Quentin chuckled and rolled off of him. "Damn, do I always get you this wet from my cum?"

Hunter was too tired to look, so he just guessed. "Yep."

"I kind of like it."

Hunter smiled and opened an eye. "For someone who wanted a blow job, you sure didn't leave me with any energy."

Quentin picked up Hunter's hand and dipped his finger into a wet spot on Hunter's stomach. "Seems you gave me a present, too."

"You came?" Hunter asked in wonder.

Quentin chuckled. "I should have known that you'd be the one to get me off that way. I hope you know how special you are."

Hunter nodded. "I do now. Now that I have you." He pulled Quentin over to him and kissed him sweetly. "But it's only because you're special, too."

Quentin smiled and ran his finger over Hunter's neck where he'd marked him. "I love you, mate."

"I love you, too." Hunter grinned at Quentin. "Mate," he said.

Then, he smiled to himself. Tomorrow, he'd break the news to Quentin on how they'd get mated the vampire way.

FORBIDDEN HUNGER SAMPLE

"Siya, I need your help in room eight."

Siya Patel looked up from the computer at the nurses' station in the emergency department to see Dr. Murphey standing in front of the counter. Friday nights in the ER were always busy.

Room eight's nurse was Scott, which meant that the doctor most likely needed a female chaperone for a pelvic exam.

"On my way," she said and followed Dr. Murphey to the room, but before they were halfway there, the doctor pulled her aside.

"I need to do an exam on a young girl who is injured and bleeding vaginally. The mother claims that the girl is seventeen, but I have my doubts. I also asked if they needed me to call the police to file a report, and the mother said absolutely not."

"What about the girl?"

"She didn't say a word. I'm hoping to pull the mother aside after the exam and speak to her privately. When we step out of the room, I'm thinking you might be able to get some information out of the girl."

"I'll do my best," Siya said, feeling heartbroken for a

teenager she hadn't even met yet.

This was why she didn't like working in the ER. Too many sad things came in. She much preferred the cardiovascular floor. Not that there weren't sad patients there, too, but it wasn't the same as seeing someone bleeding everywhere from a car accident or a guy who had gotten his face punched in during a fight. Or in this case, a possible rape victim with a mother who didn't want her daughter to report it. Siya had seen it before. It had ended up being the stepfather, and that was why the mother hadn't wanted to press charges. It made Siya sick to think about.

A young girl who didn't look any older than fifteen lay on the bed with a woman standing next to her. The girl looked frightened and unsure, but the woman looked angry and irritated, and right away, Siya knew things were worse off than what the doctor suspected.

"Hannah," the doctor said to the patient, "this is Nurse Siya. She's going to stay in here and help me while I do your exam, okay?"

Hannah looked at her mother and then back to the doctor and nodded.

"Siya, this is Hannah and her mom, Jane," Dr. Murphey said.

Siya managed a fake smile. "Hello."

"Let's get started, shall we?" the doctor said.

As he gave Hannah instructions and told her what to expect, Siya studied the two females and wondered what the hell they were doing in a human hospital.

Because these two were shifters. Siya was ninety-nine percent sure of it. She didn't know enough to know if they were cat- or wolf-shifters, but thanks to her best friend, she knew they weren't fully human.

Her best friend, Demi, was half-cat-shifter and had lived her life in secret until about nine months ago when she had been injured and had no choice but to reach out to the local cat-shifters. Before that, Siya had known only Demi, but since then, she had met many more shifters and could recognize them now. She couldn't put her finger on it, but there was something about them that made them different from humans.

Now, she knew that shifters had their own hospital with their own doctors. They wouldn't come to a human hospital unless they wanted to hide something.

Like the fact that this *Jane*—or whatever her real name was—was not Hannah's mother. They looked very different from each other and were too close in age. There was, of course, adoption, and shifters aged more slowly, but adoption didn't seem to happen often in the shifter community. Also, Jane didn't once reach out and hold her supposed daughter's hand despite the young girl obviously being scared.

The doctor motioned Siya to come closer to him.

"I'm going to need a suture kit," he said in a low voice, and Siya momentarily closed her eyes.

This poor girl must be in a ton of pain if she needed to be stitched up.

Siya straightened and looked at Jane. The woman was on her phone, too busy to pay attention to what was wrong. Or she was pretending to be distracted. Siya had best remember that Jane had better hearing than she and Dr. Murphey combined.

Siya went to the door and stuck her head out to ask for the supplies the doctor needed since she was required to stay in the hospital room until the pelvic exam was done.

"I'm just going to check you for STIs—or STDs, as you might call them."

Jane smirked at her phone, and Siya knew they wouldn't find anything since shifters couldn't catch sexually transmitted infections or diseases.

Once the doctor finished with his exam, he made sure

Hannah was comfortable and asked Jane to go to a private room reserved for family members for when the doctor needed to discuss issues that shouldn't be talked about in front of certain patients, like minors or elderly who could no longer take care of themselves. Thankfully, it worked because if it were any other seventeen-year-old patient, the doctor would speak to both her and the mother in the same room.

The second they were out of the room, Siya pulled up the doctor's stool and moved to the side of Hannah's bed.

"Hey, Hannah, you know that we're here to help you, right?"

"Yeah," she said uncertainly.

"Is there anything at all you'd like to share with me?"

She hesitated, and for a second, Siya hoped she'd get something out of the girl, but Hannah just shook her head.

Siya chewed on her bottom lip. She needed another approach. Hannah needed to know she could trust her.

"Do you have any pets?"

"No. No pets."

"That's too bad. I have two pets. I have a huge cat named Vance and a large dog named Damien, who almost looks like a wolf."

Hannah's eyes widened to the point Siya thought they might pop out of her head.

"Some people think my names are odd, but both of my pets are fearless leaders in their own right, and I think their names are fitting." Siya kept her voice casual, as if she really were talking about pets she owned.

"What about you?" she asked. "Do you like cats or dogs better?"

Hannah licked her lips nervously. "Um...I like cats." Her hand shook as she pointed to the door to her room. "But my mom likes dogs."

"That's interesting." So, Hannah was a cat-shifter, and her

fake mom was a wolf-shifter. "Hey, do you want to see some pictures of my pets?"

"Yes, please."

Siya pulled her phone out of her pocket and brought up her Notes app. She rapidly typed, asking if Hannah was her real name.

She showed her the screen. "What do you think? Does he look scary?"

"*No*, he looks nice."

Hannah wasn't her name.

Siya took her phone back and quickly entered another question, asking if Jane was the real name of the older woman.

"What about this picture? Do you think my dog looks silly?"

"*No*, he looks kind of mean in that photo."

Siya nodded and took her phone back, swiftly erasing her messages before "Jane" came back.

But if she could find out Hannah's real name before that happened, she would feel so much better. Jane's real name would be good to have, too, but she didn't know how much time they had.

She supposed she could have Hannah type her name in herself, but she was scared what Jane would do if she walked in and saw that Hannah was on Siya's phone. It was easier to pretend like she was showing the young girl pictures.

"So, are you sure you don't have any pets?" she asked, hoping that Hannah would understand the question. "Because now that I told you my pets' names, you could tell me yours."

"Oh, um, I used to have a cat. Her name was *Emery Telfort*, but she ran away, and I haven't seen her since." Hannah—or rather Emery—started crying. "I think she really misses home."

"Oh, honey," Siya whispered. "I'm sure your cat will make it back home and soon."

She sniffled. "You think so?"

"I do."

Siya was at the counter to grab a tissue when the door opened and Jane walked in.

"What's going on here?" Jane's eyes bounced from Hannah to her and back to Hannah.

Siya could see the alarm in the other woman's eyes, and she didn't want her to panic and do anything stupid.

Bringing the tissue back to her patient, Siya said, "Nothing. Your daughter is in a lot of pain, and Dr. Murphey has yet to prescribe her any medication."

He had numbed the area he sewed up, but Siya was sure Hannah really was in pain. Or she would be once the lidocaine wore off.

"Oh, yes, I meant to do that." He looked at Hannah. "I'm so sorry about that."

Hannah sniffled. "It's okay."

Dr. Murphey signed in to the computer. "I'll order that right now, and a nurse will bring it in."

While Jane watched him, Siya quickly took a picture of her since her cell was still in her hand. She had no idea if she'd gotten a good angle, but she prayed she'd gotten something identifiable as she slipped it into her pocket.

The doctor looked up and over at Siya. "Thank you for your help, Siya."

"You're welcome." She turned to Hannah. "I hope you feel better soon."

"Thank you."

She headed to the door as Jane narrowed her eyes at Siya, but she wasn't going to let herself be intimidated. She knew bigger and badder shifters than her. Plus, it wasn't her first day as a nurse. She could handle threatening looks any day.

As soon as she exited, she rushed to a break room and pulled out her phone.

ABOUT THE AUTHOR

R.L. Kenderson is two best friends writing under one name.

Renae has always loved reading, and in third grade, she wrote her first poem where she learned she might have a knack for this writing thing. Lara remembers sneaking her grandmother's Harlequin novels when she was probably too young to be reading them, and since then, she knew she wanted to write her own.

When they met in college, they bonded over their love of reading and the TV show *Charmed*. What really spiced up their friendship was when Lara introduced Renae to romance novels. When they discovered their first vampire romance, they knew there would always be a special place in their hearts for paranormal romance. After being unable to find certain storylines and characteristics they wanted to read about in the hundreds of books they consumed, they decided to write their own.

One lives in the Minneapolis-St. Paul area and the other in the Kansas City area where they're a sonographer/stay-at-home mom/wife and pharmacist/mother by day, and together they're a sexy author by night. They communicate through phone, email, and whole lot of messaging.

You can find them at http://www.rlkenderson.com, Facebook, Instagram, TikTok, Twitter, and Goodreads. Join their reader group! Or you can email them at rlkenderson@rlkenderson.com, or sign up for their newsletter. They always love hearing from their readers.